Gail Rayner trained as a nurse in Exeter and lives and still practises in Plymouth. A family of six children now grown up, Gail has a bit of time on her hands. This is the second book based on her local area.

Gail Rayner

THE LADY

AUSTIN MACAULEY PUBLISHERS™

LONDON • CAMBRIDGE • NEW YORK • SHARJAH

A CIP catalogue record for this title is available from the British Library.

ISBN 9781787102347 (Paperback)
ISBN 9781787102354 (E-Book)

www.austinmacauley.com

First Published (2018)
Austin Macauley Publishers Ltd
25 Canada Square
Canary Wharf
London
E14 5LQ

Inspiration found in Charlestown and encouragement from family and friends.

Chapter One

The elder man stood looking out of the window at the two children playing, smiling to himself. "Cooper, when my wife passed, I feared for Elizabeth but with yourself and your family's help, she is growing up a bright happy child, if a little headstrong." He flinched as she poked her opponent in the abdomen, shouting something about pirates and waving the little wooden sword they were using. Her opponent rolled over on the grass in an exaggerated manner, holding his stomach and moaning. She stopped in her tracks, looking concerned. She was about to poke him again with her sword when he got up laughing and jumping around, all forgiven as he chased after her, swishing the grass with his sword. Around and around the tree, both children went laughing.

Turning around to face Cooper he chose his words carefully.

"I am not well! I charge you with the duty of taking care of my daughter. She will have her governess, and of course our solicitor Mr Allen; she is high-spirited and has a talent for finding trouble." Turning again to face the window, he took a shallow breath as a wave of pain came again. In a raspy voice, "Protect her please," said he, taking a breath and looking back at his friend, confidant and gamekeeper. "She is like her mother (a knowing look passed between the two men) and this will be her making or destruction." Now turning back once more to face the craggy, once handsome face of his friend, his hand held out, they shook hands.

"Yes, milord, we will."

Twelve years later.

"Don't spare the truth, Mr Allen. I need to know, what does this mean for my children and me?'

"Of course I am sorry for your loss, Milady." She gave him a look of impatience. "Umm... umm... well, you are nearly broke, your mortgage is paid, and no male heir to inherit, but I do not know how much money is in the bank..." His voice trailed off. Sitting in the morning room, her hands clasped on her lap, she was prepared for the worst. On a brighter note, at least the house was not in the bank's grasp.

She looked down at her hands. "How did we get in such a state?" She already knew.

"Lord Tremaine gambled unwisely and..." He hesitated and blushed. She looked up at this dear family friend and solicitor.

"I know about 'her' in town; how does she fare in all this?"

"I believe she has already moved on."

"Clever girl, Survival!" *The whore,* she thought to herself, but at least she kept him away from her bed. She couldn't remember the last time they even slept in the same room.

"You must speak to the bank manager; I can do it for you if you wish." He glanced at the horrified look on her face.

"No. I will, although the thought of having to speak to him makes my flesh crawl." He smiled. "I know, but he might be a useful ally."

The wind blew inland making the sea rough and treacherous. *Summer is nearly gone and autumn is coming,* she thought as she brought her coat up around her neck. She shuddered, just catching her hat before it blew away. Mama always said I should wear ribbons to keep my hat on.

She was walking along the road near the harbour; seagulls all around, people shouting to each other, and that smell of fish.

Heading for the dreaded bank and the appointment she'd been dreading, the tall grey stone building was as daunting on the outside as her business was inside.

"Lady Tremaine, sorry for your loss!" Touching his hat in respect was a passer-by who knew of her but she couldn't recall him. She smiled a thank-you. She'd been like this for a few weeks, having to face up to the desolation she now found herself in. Taking a deep breath and holding her chin high, she entered the bank and headed towards the bank teller.

"I have an appointment with Mr Smith."

"Yes. Name, please." The teller was looking down at some papers and did not look up at the woman's voice.

"Lady Tremaine." The young man now looked up and, feeling awkward at his curtness, said, "Would you care to take a seat?" Coming out from behind his desk, he led the way to three little chairs with a circular table. "I will inform the manager that you are here," he said, giving an awkward head nod. She didn't notice; her thoughts were of what more bad news she might hear.

A chubby older man appeared in the nearby doorway. "Lady Tremaine! Sorry to keep you waiting." Walking towards her, holding out his hand, he kissed her now ungloved hand with a wet kiss. She pulled her hand away subtly.

"Morning Mr Smith, I have some urgent business to discuss."

"Of course! This way," said he, leading the way to his big bright office, standing to one side and allowing her to enter the room.

"Mr Smith, my husband's will has been read now. I need to know the state of my account, please."

"Yes, yes; pray take a seat," sitting down in the much more comfortable chair than the hard little chair on the other side of the door. "As you already know, there is a need for concern, your mortgage is paid, your father saw to that, and the property is not entailed to a male relative?" said he, raising his eyebrows.

"No, there are no male relatives except for my son, but he is too young," said she, letting out a sigh.

"But not much of anything else left; that is until spring with your crops and of course the pilchard fishing."

"Did Lord Tremaine make any allowance for his lady friend?" If he was embarrassed, he didn't show it.

"No, apparently not, I believe she is self-sufficient."

"Probably with the money he had already given her."

"I could not say," said he, looking down at the papers sitting innocently on his desk.

"So how can I assist you, Milady?" he asked, with plenty of evincing on the assist.

Now the creepy bit comes, she thought, *fight or run!* So she gave him 'the look' instead, enough to stop any sensible man at fifty yards; it would seem he was not the sensible sort!

He got up and walked around the table. "I am sure we could come to some sort of arrangement." He was going to put his hand on her shoulder; she jumped up, taking him by surprise. He, momentarily taken aback, regained composure. "Umm, you could sell your farm cottages, but it's a bad time of year to do so."

"I have no intention of getting rid of my tenants!"

Looking into her face he walked back behind the safety of his desk.

"Thank you for your help," said she, looking him squarely in the face. "So how much money do I actually have at the moment?"

Looking down at the 'innocent' papers he rustled through them. "Ahh, about two thousand pounds."

"That little!" she didn't mean to say out loud, walking towards the door. "I'll shall draw half now. Can you instruct the cashier, please?" Looking dismayed at such a sum going out in one lump, carried by a woman alone, he said, "Milady, these roads are not safe!"

Knowing his meaning, "I will be safe!" said she, putting her chin up in defiance.

She walked towards the door; he got up from behind the desk and was at the door knob, holding it with his sticky hand, probably from nervous sweat, before she could reach it. She glared at him. "Thank you, Mr Smith!" His previous intentions were of an un-gentlemanly nature, thinking her a poor widow, not this strong woman in front of him.

We will survive, but not that way, she thought to herself, trying not to shudder.

She was glad he didn't pursue what was showing in his eyes. Her fist was hidden behind her handbag; she thought it was going to be put to use; she hadn't punched anyone since her husband, then she wiped the memory from her current thoughts. I have more to think about now, that part of my life is over.

He bowed slightly, keeping his eyes on her as though he did not quite trust her. He ushered her out of the door towards the cashier who had just finished serving a customer. Mr Smith handed a piece of paper to the young man whose eyes widened; he looked up and smiled at Milady. She smiled back but felt uneasy. *I must check my pistol,* she thought, *before I travel back home.*

Business completed she went towards the stable where her horse was tied up. Feeling uneasy she looked around, getting her pistol out of her bag to check it still had its contents. She didn't hear someone come in behind her.

"Morning!"

"Oh!" She jumped, annoyed with herself for being caught off guard.

He looked down at her hand. "Planning on shooting someone, are we, Milady?"

Composure now regained she said, "Do you make it a habit of walking up behind a lady? I do not shoot unless a person deserves it or gets in my way!"

He looked concerned. "I presume you are worried about the highwayman that has been seen around these parts?" There was something reassuring about his face. He caught her staring at it.

"Yes. About reports that he is around."

"He! Could be a woman."

"You're playing with me, sir! Reports are of a muscularly built man, not a woman. Anyway, I must be on my way." He came forward to help her mount. "It is all right, I can manage." She slipped her foot into the stirrup and hoisted herself up onto her horse, who neighed softly. "Good boy!" she said, smoothing his neck, and, "Goodbye, sir," giving him a sideways look, sitting astride the horse in a very unladylike fashion, but it was safer if one had a need to gallop. She waved to the stable boy who acknowledged her with a smile as Star gently cantered out of the stable.

A handsome man! Mm, I wonder where he is from. A strange accent, and who is he? Enough of fanciful thoughts, I must keep my mind on the task at hand.

The wind was now turning it into a tiring and dangerous ride. Mama, I really should have listened to you, she reflected as she put her hood over her bonnet. She heard hooves coming up behind her. She peeked over her shoulder, her worst fears were realised as a black-coated figure was coming up behind her. He was shouting something.

"Ha, I don't think so!" Not knowing what he'd said, but it wasn't hallo, she crouched down. "Come on, boy," she cried, digging her heels in the side of her horse who knew immediately what to do, and like a spring from a trap he sped off, she crouching down behind his head and blending in with his body contours, her bag tucked in between them. But the other rider had had a good start and was catching them up fast. Her breathing was shallow, barely daring to look around, she caught a glimpse of a coat and a hand reaching out for her hood. She moved her head to one side; he missed but was not distracted. The hooves of both animals thundered along the uneven road. Fumbling in her coat she fired her little pistol, aiming at his leg; he was shocked, he moaned! His horse lost its momentum and fell back, while she continued to speed as if her horse's tail was on fire. They didn't stop till they galloped into the courtyard.

The sound of a galloping horse brought the stable hand Dan and Ernest out in time to see Milady about to fall off the horse. Both rushed to her aid and caught her; she, landing in their arms with an "Ooh, thank you!", held on to Ernest and looked over his shoulder to the path. There was no sign of her assailant.

Getting her composure back she slipped out of his arms, unsteadily landing on her feet. She brushed her hair from her face, and looking at the stable boy said, "Take care of Star and check him over, please." She watched Dan walking away, smoothing the horse's mane and saying soothing words into his ear.

Now she was composed. "Milady, what happened?" She looked into his concerned face. "It was the highwayman, wasn't it?"

"Yes, I think so. Your teaching all those years ago might have just saved us. I shot him, so he will be limping. But why me? I drew money out of the bank, no one knew, except Mr Smith and the bank teller! Was it them or an opportune attempted robbery?"

Ernest was deep in thought. "Leave it with me. I will make enquiries."

"Ernest! Do not do anything foolish. I need you here, not in the Truro cells, or worse, dead. Look this way, please," said she, tossing him a tight bundle. He caught it.

"How much?"

"One thousand pounds."

Smiling at her worried face he said, "Trust me, Milady!" and raised his eyebrows in a cheeky fashion. They laughed and she looked after him as he walked away.

"Now what's he up to?" she said quietly to herself. Matilda the nanny with Charles on her hip and holding Amelia's hand met her at the door. "Ooh, Milady, are you all right?"

"Mama!" Her arms out, the little blonde-haired girl ran to her mother's arms, Milady picked her up and snuggled her, holding her tight. She suddenly realised how fragile life was, and how she could have lost hers today. She must be more careful; what would have become of them?

Fighting back the tears, "Come on now little ones, let your mother breathe!" Matilda steered the two children indoors. As she looked after them a tear rolled down her face, and she wiped it away quickly.

"Matilda, I will be up shortly to read to them." She went indoors to her husband's study and looked around. "Now what am I looking for?" She poured herself a large brandy and taking a sip murmured, "Mmm, nice!" and sat down behind the big oak table. Running her hands along the grain of the wood she felt melancholy for her childhood, growing up in this old house. Looking into the crystal glass she exclaimed, "How do we afford brandy?" In shock, she sat bolt upright and started opening the desk drawers, lots and lots of papers, she was reading them and flinging them all over the floor; she didn't know what she was looking for, but she would know when she found it.

The floor was covered with receipts, letters—personal and business—but none for brandy, in fact not for several of their luxury food items. Silk for her last ball gown, where did that come from? There were more questions than answers.

Ernest knocked as he walked in, someone had tipped him off that Milady was on the rampage in the study.

Looking at Ernest she realised he knew what she was going to ask. He looked uncomfortable, thinking of his next words carefully.

"Milady, what are you doing?" He spread his arms out as if to sweep all the papers up.

"Ernest, we have been friends since childhood! The truth… I cannot deal with it if I do not know what 'it' is."

"Smuggling! Just a little for personal use."

"I had no idea! I have been living in a little soft nest with my children! Who is in charge of all this?"

"How come we haven't got in trouble for this?" she continued, waving a paper around, "and the highwayman? Any news, and is my horse all right?" trying not to smile at her own outburst. Looking at his dear face they both smiled together. "Well, Ernest, it was a shock; is there anything else I should know before I find it out?"

Ernest looked pensive. "Nothing to deal with at the moment, Milady."

"You sure while I am in the mood, is there anything else I need to know?" looking down at the papers over her lap and the floor, bending forward as if to gather all the papers up. "Well, Ernest, enlighten me now," looking up in anticipation.

"Matilda and I want to get married." Looking up he held his breath waiting for the outburst laughing.

"I know. That's been coming for a while," said Milady as she beamed looking up at Ernest.

"I thought you might have been annoyed, under one roof and all!"

"I know, it's unconventional, I am happy for you both, will you stay here?"

Looking shocked he said, "Oh Milady, no plans to leave you and the little ones!"

Looking into his face she replied, "That's good. Congratulations, have you set the date yet?"

"No, we will get this business resolved first. I have asked around. No one has seen a limping man, but probably he is not walking too well to be out and about. The militia know, but not about the pistol firing."

"Well, at least he won't be attacking anyone else. So from whom does this come?" said she, holding up her glass and taking a large sip, then remembering she promised to read to the children in a while. *I'd better slow down with this,* she thought, putting the glass down.

Approaching her and kneeling on the floor in front of her, "I need to speak to someone first." She looked into his face giving him the little smile she has done since a child, normally getting her own way, but not this time.

"They are desperate, dangerous men, not ones to cross. Please don't look at me like that, it's for your own safety!' He was now looking like the elder brother and not her servant.

"All right, I understand" came from her mouth but her brain was working overtime.

Later, after Ernest had gone out, the light now quickly fading, she took a candle and looked into the flame. *I suppose we'll be using tallow candles soon,* she thought. Lifting her skirts with her free hand and quietly going towards the children's room, she could hear Matilda talking. She pushed the door open.

"Mama!"

"Hello my darlings! Good night," she said, smiling at Mattie, as the children called her, "I will look after them now. Off you go."

The nanny, looking tired and relieved, did a little curtsy. "Night, Milady."

"Say night to Mattie."

"Night," said a sleepy little girl. Charles was already asleep.

"What story tonight?" asked a mother looking adoringly at her child, not believing they could have created someone so beautiful. A sleepy little girl looked up through heavy eyelashes, and said, "Margery book."

"So 'Goody Two-Shoes' it is then." Again she thought, I must not invite her to choose, as it is the same book every night. Opening the book at where she left it last night, Milady was getting into the story when she heard gentle breathing; the little blonde-haired girl was fast asleep. Sweeping a stray ringlet off the little girl's forehead she kissed it gently, got off the bed and tiptoed to the window, nearly tripping over Charles's animal toy. Trying to stifle a giggle she pulled the curtains back to look at the full moon. The lawn looked menacing with the shadows flickering across the grass, the birds noisy and some unknown predator chasing its prey which was putting up a fight, it seemed, with all the screeching going on.

Ernest cannot be in yet, the peacocks aren't out, she thought. A figure appeared on the lawn looking up at her. Her heart racing she exclaimed, "My Lord, it's not Ernest! Where's my pistol!" As quick as the figure came he went. Her nerves now heightened, and hearing a door going somewhere, she rushed out of the bedroom, this time

16

jumping over children's obstacles, ran into her bedroom looking around for a weapon of some sort. Ahh, the bed warmer! It wasn't hot but she could give a heavy whack with it. She crept along the landing, going down the stairs, and raised it to attack the person walking along the corridor. He turned around in time; it was Ernest putting his hands up in defence. She lowered the pan and the cold coals dropped to the floor, holding her chest she cried, "You scared me!"

He gave her a reassuring hug. "I am sorry."

"I thought you'd all be asleep!" said he, bursting into laughter at what would have been an awful commotion, "Milady knocks out her faithful friend, all around the village tomorrow."

Someone else in the house stirred. Matilda appeared looking dishevelled, with stick in her hand ready for action. "What is it with you ladies?" said Ernest, laughing but proud of them both.

"Well, there be folk around here that mean us harm!" said a breathless Matilda.

"Thank you both!"

All now looking at the pan in her hands, the three stood there smiling. Ernest took control. "Right, the stables are secure, Dan is on guard, I was in the middle of checking the doors and windows." Ernest kicked the coals to one side, making a mental note to pick them up when the house was settled.

Milady looked at Mattie. "Come with me, we'll check the big office, I don't want to go on my own." She holding the pan up and Mattie with her stick went the other way to Ernest. Picking up a candle on the way, they went into the study. It was how she'd left it, untidy but the same. Pulling the curtains back she saw the French window was open; the air outside brushed her skin. "Mattie, look!" Shoulder to shoulder they looked outside. "I don't remember opening the door; inside quick, time for peacocks on the lawn, and where's Hugo?"

"Are you both all right?" They both visibly jumped. "Ooh, sorry."

"The window was open!"

Ernest looked concerned. "You both go to the kitchen. Hugo's in there."

"I wondered where he was." An Irish wolfhound was not a quiet dog. "How's his paw?"

"Well, now thorn's out."

"I wondered why he didn't bark. Is he well enough to get up and about?"

"Yes."

"Let him walk around the house, if there's an intruder he'll find them."

The two women, different in background but both equally scared, walked along the corridor to the kitchen where Hugo raised his head, getting up when he saw his mistress; limping a little but able to walk. "I didn't shoot you, did I?" she said, smoothing the dog's head and bending as if to tell him a secret. "Come on boy, let's check the house." She picked up a candle.

"Milady, shouldn't you wait here? Ernest said we should…"

Interrupting Matilda her mistress said, "But I have Hugo with me. Tell him we are checking upstairs first, especially the children's room." Picking up her pan she wandered down the corridor, looking braver than she felt. Walking quietly up the stairs every step seemed to creak. Hugo looked up at his mistress as if to say *ssh*. Reaching the top of the stairs they turned left towards the children's room, Hugo quietly sniffing as he went. The children were still asleep in the same position as she had left them. She let out a sigh of relief and they worked their way along the corridor. Hugo started to growl. "What is it, boy?" said she, still holding his collar. He started to pull now, the growl became a bark, louder and louder, he got away from Milady and dashed into her bedroom, barking under the bed.

Ernest appeared with his shotgun. Pulling Hugo away was no mean feat now he was snarling and ready to attack the intruder.

"Who's there?" A *meow* rang out.

"A cat, Milady," said Mattie, nervously laughing.

Ernest was not so convinced. "Come out, make it easier on yourself or I'll let the dog have you!"

A thin man crawled out. Ernest pointed his gun at him, "Who are you and why are you here?"

"I came to see the mistress. I got in. then I heard that dog and I ended up here to hide."

"Why?"

"The master, he gets brandy from us and, he's overdue payment." Milady's eyes went to the ceiling.

"This is for an unpaid bill?"

"Yes, Milady."

"How much?" He handed over a piece of paper on which £100 was written.

"Where is your master?"

"Can't tell, I don't know real master, only one that I talks to and he'd kill us!"

"Why didn't you just knock on the door?"

"Don't know, Milady."

"I'll meet him."

"No, Milady, I'll go," said Ernest.

"No I will, tomorrow morning on the beach, by the path at dawn." He went to argue.

"That is my final answer. Let him go, Ernest, but see him off the grounds, please, and let those damned birds out!"

He looked at her, then biting his tongue he looked at the man. "This way, you!" said he, pointing at the door.

"That man has been in my house while my children sleep! Doesn't bear thinking about. Luckily he doesn't appear to be that sort of man."

Silence. Mattie and Milady looked at each other. "I'll sleep in the babies' room tonight, Milady.'

"Yes, good idea, thank you!" said she, touching Mattie's arm in gratitude. "I don't think Hugo will settle tonight."

"Right, to bed. I am up early. I will speak to the staff when I come back from the beach."

Ernest came back in. "Peacocks are out. I've told Dan what happened, and to be vigilant, but I think we are safe for the moment."

"Did my husband keep receipts?"

"Yes."

"So where? Let's make sure this person is not trying to rob us."

Ernest led the way into the study. He moved books off the shelf to show a folder full of sums.

He opened it up to the latest entry. "Yes, he did owe that sum, so tomorrow we will go to the beach. Get some sleep. Tomorrow could be a hard day." Feeling scared but excited at the same time, *I must put an end to this,* she thought as she climbed the stairs for the second time that night, this time at a leisurely pace. She could hear Hugo walking around upstairs. No one was getting in while his senses were heightened.

Chapter Two

Fretful sleep, tossing and turning, mind full of pirates, swords and screaming, waking with a jump, straining her ears, hearing every creak on the stairs; but Milady was reassured as Hugo had the freedom of the house. He was finally asleep on the landing snoring very loudly, so he felt secure. Wiping the sweat from her face she lay back down and drifted into a settled sleep. She was up before dawn washing in cold water poured from her jug into a bowl in her bedroom. She chose bland plain clothes and an old brown coat for the occasion, not wanting to draw attention to herself. Tying her dark hair up high to go under a hat, she went down into the kitchen and put the cauldron on the coals for hot water. Sitting down at the table, she got her pistol out of her bag. Blowing into the barrel she said to herself, "You need a good clean, but not now," then wiping the flint area, "if you fail me I could be..."

"Could be what?" said Ernest. Milady jumped. "Stop making me jump!" she said with a smile.

"Ahh! Expecting some gun action, are we?"

"I have to be vigilant, there are strange folk about that wish us harm," said she smiling. "According to your dear wife-to-be!"

"You are not going alone, and no arguing! I'll be around, you can do the talking, but if it doesn't go to plan; well, I am there."

She looked down at the table. "Yes, you're right. I should not go alone, but be discreet."

"Am I not always? Is your gun clean?"

"Yes."

"You have powder and ramrod?"

"Yes, I've loaded it, I feel like a child!" said she, laughing.

"You have been my pupil."

"Yes, and I am grateful for your knowledge and loyalty." Mrs West came rushing in, tying her apron around her ample body.

"Ooh sorry, overslept me dears!" She looked down at the pistol and then at Milady's face, as if to ask the question. Milady and Ernest looked at each other and smiled. "Ooh thanks, whoever put the water on," she added, looking at Ernest.

"Wasn't me, was Milady!" Mrs West now looked embarrassed.

"It is all right. I was first up and I haven't forgotten how to heat water," said Milady, putting her arms around Mrs West's shoulders. "Come on Ernest, nearly sunrise," she continued, putting her pistol in her pocket upright so the powder and ball didn't fall out, with powder and the small ramrod, getting an anxious look from Cook. "Tell Matilda we will not be long." She was trying to give herself courage.

Ernest picked up his larger version and they were gone. The beach was a few yards from the end of the lawn, the other side of the large wrought iron fence. It would have been a useful place if they were involved in smuggling. Approaching the path they unlocked the gate; it creaked as it was pushed.

"Can't surprise anyone, can we!" said Ernest.

"'Morning to you both! I do like prompt customers. If it makes you feel any better, I saw you leave your house, so you couldn't surprise me." Ernest was restless holding his gun tight.

"It's all right, my man! No violence, just payment and I'll be on my way." The man, wearing foreign-looking dirty clothes spoke with an accent similar to the stranger from the day before. They did not recognise him, he had teeth missing, and if they were down wind he was probably smelly, too.

"No more business with us!" spoke Milady, feeling angry that her husband had done business with the likes of him, putting them all in danger. She handed him the money.

"All right, Milady!" said he, pretending to bow. As he jumped forward to grab her a shot rang out.

"That's enough of that, be on your way!" A tall man dressed in a large woollen coat and a large-brimmed hat came from nowhere. The smuggler seemed afraid of him. "Now take your money and go; leave these good people alone or you'll get a whipping!"

Ernest lent forward. "Was that your gun again?"

"No, I didn't get a chance! Just as well. I was aiming at his legs but I think I would have got his—" she pointed to the top of his legs. Ernest was looking puzzled, then the halfpenny dropped.

Laughing, he said, "Just as well you didn't shoot!"

"Thank you sir, for your assistance." He looked directly at her, stopping her dead in her tracks. "You, we met in the stable!"

"Yes we did." He put his hand out and nodded. "Charles Long, Milady, I am your neighbour.

Holding onto her gloved hand longer than society allowed, "This is my friend Ernest," reluctantly taking her hand away, looking at both men.

He put his hand out to Ernest; they shook, the greeting crossed the class barrier. If Ernest felt it, he didn't show any emotion.

"So why out so early?"

"Charles, call me Charles. I was walking the dog, and taking in fresh air. I love this time of the morning." A hunting dog came bounding over. "I won't hold you up any longer!" he said, nodding towards Milady and Ernest, and walked off towards the beach.

They watched him go. "Where did that other fellow go?" said Ernest. Both were looking around.

"I don't know. I wonder why he was going to grab me? He wasn't limping," said she, looking towards the house.

"I dread to think, but it wouldn't have been for a good reason. A bit desperate, though," said Ernest, looking concerned.

They walked across the lawn; the grass was damp with dew. The daytime bird kingdom was awake, chirping and flying above their heads, warning others of the human proximity, not knowing that the humans were more concerned about another human being and his whereabouts. Milady's coat was flapping in the breeze, her blouse open at the neck; she was feeling hot with foreboding!

The house was waking up. Hugo was racing around, barking at anything that moved, he made the atmosphere light, making all that saw him laugh.

At the front door stood Mattie (with a look of thunder) and Tabitha who had the children in their arms. Mattie, looking concerned, said, "A bit early to walk the dog!"

Ernest stopped in front of Matilda, putting a protective arm out, "Go inside and I'll explain what happened," turning around, looking out over the lawn, "where is that damn dog?" With that, Hugo bounded up, stopping for a bit of affection then shaking his wet fur. "Ahh," said a now wet Milady, "Hugo!"

All went inside, chatting as they brushed their clothes off, heading towards the kitchen.

Dark eyes watched them from the beach path. He continued to walk with his dog to his cottage.

"So that's where she lives," said he, smiling.

The children were sitting at the table, eating bread and butter with their favourite jam that Mrs West made from the garden fruit, which was plentiful this year. From deep thought, Milady stirred. "I think I'll take bread and jam down to the cottages later, and have a talk with the tenants."

Ernest looking up said, "Yes, I'll go with you, I have to talk to the man about materials."

Charles, hardly big enough to sit at the table, had Matilda standing behind him ready to pounce if he fell. "Come on now, young man, eat up and we can play in your play room!" It was really the conservatory but had the most light and warmth from the sun. Smiling a red jammy smile at her, Charles handed her a squashed handful of bread, butter and jam. "Thank you!" she said, taking it gingerly from his hands. Matilda looking up saw her mistress watching from the doorway. "Milady, you shouldn't be standing drinking your tea."

"I wanted to see the children before we went out walking."

In the busy kitchen, even Dan the stable boy was having his bread and cheese before his day's work. Later Tabitha would take his dinner out to him, probably more bread and cheese, with cold turkey 'leftovers' from last night, and an apple. It's going to be a long winter, Milady thought to herself, looking at the merry little group that had become her family. Fortunately her husband had no male siblings to claim her family home under the unfair inheritance law. I think I would have shot them if there was anyone, or married them… that thought brought her back to the present and reality.

"Milady, are you ready?"

Looking up at Ernest, she said, "Oh yes, I'll get my coat," going to the table and kissing both children on their heads. "Matilda, keep outside doors locked, and Dan, keep your eyes open, please. Let Hugo have the run of the house." Matilda was now looking worried.

Ernest touched her shoulder. "I won't be long, love. It's just a precaution."

"Yes, I know this whole smuggler thing worries ee."

Ernest and Milady left the house going to the stable to saddle their horses. "Do you think we should leave them?" said she, looking back at the house.

"It's you the smuggler wanted, but our mysterious neighbour scared him off."

"Yes, what's his accent? I did not recognise it."

"I think he's American but trying to conceal his accent a little."

Looking at Ernest she said, "It's been about five years since the end of their war of independence."

"Yes, but you know how folks are, scared of their own shadows."

"Yes true, they have reason to be at times... Quite handsome though," she not meaning to say it out loud.

Realising and laughing, she looked at Ernest who was smiling.

It was a dry day, no sign of rain, a gentle breeze making this a pleasant ride. Ernest kept looking around. "You don't think anyone's around, do you?" she asked Ernest as he was obviously ill at ease.

"No, but we must be careful." They pulled up at the neat little row of houses, which were a hive of activity. Ernest had already got word to them about the impending visit by Milady with a view to mending the houses ready for winter.

"Milady."

Nodding his head and removing his cap, Matthew the spokesman came forward as Ernest helped her off her horse. "The houses look in need of repair! Do you think with the farm work as well you can get them ready for the cold weather?"

"We will, Milady. It's going to be a hard one, I'm thinking."

"I think you're right. Has Ernest told you about the smugglers that are around?" He was looking uncomfortable.

"Yes Milady." She, looking at Matthew and puzzled, was suddenly distracted on hearing her name.

"Ooh, Milady!" A young woman came out of the cottage looking very much with child. Milady walked towards the young woman and placed a gentle hand on the obvious growing belly.

"Not long now, Lottie."

"Yes Milady, thank you for the things you sent down, they are lovely and will keep littlings warm."

"You're welcome, Lottie."

Ernest was already at work making a list of materials. "I'll take some men into town for the items we need."

"All right, be careful," said she, handing out the preserves, bread and other produce from Mrs West's kitchen. "She always cooks for an army." The food was given out to the women to share between themselves. Milady was restless to get back to the children.

"Right, I'm going back."

"Be careful, there's a strange man around."

"Pardon, Milady, shouldn't you be waiting till the men come back?"

"I have my gun. I'll be safe." Getting back on her horse she waved to the little group, who were talking amongst themselves as they waved back. Setting off to the house along the beach road she looked out to sea, so rough and so free.

"Hello!" A man jumped out and grabbed her horse's reins. Taken by surprise she raised her hand to hit him. It was the man from the morning.

"Get off me!" She was holding on tight to the reins; in the confusion the horse threatened to bolt, the man was grabbing for her body, her mind went blank, survival paramount. She kicked him, he was momentarily stunned then grabbed her leg. Fumbling in her bag for her pistol she got it out and aimed it at him. "Get off my horse!" said she, calmly and uncaring.

"Come on now, Milady, let's be friends!" He let go of her leg. "Does your master know you're out?"

"I do what I want."

"Where are you from?" said she.

"Louisiana, and I am not answerable to the likes of you English!" He came closer and she lifted her arm up.

"I will shoot!" He lunged, she fired, he looked at her like a rabbit caught in a trap and staggered, clutching his chest and fell onto his back. The smell of blood made Star rear up and gallop over the path the wrong way. She couldn't catch her breath but she held on to the reins or mane, she didn't know which. She was aware of a horse beside her, she didn't know whether to hit out or not, then she realised it was the 'nice face' man.

He pulled her horse to a halt. "There boy!" patting the panting horse.

Catching her breath, "Thank you sir!" she said. "I shot a man back there. I don't know if he's dead, I am not sure what he was going to do but I don't think it was good." He took the pistol out of her hand.

"Now then, it's all right. Let's get you indoors," said he, leading her horse to his cottage and lifting her down. "Agnes!" he shouted. A woman in an apron appeared at the door. "Help please!" Milady had fainted; lifting her up he took her indoors to the parlour and laid her on the chaise longue. "Stay with her, Agnes!" He rushed back out, and leaping on his horse he rode off. Milady woke up, looking around.

"Where am I?"

"You're in the master's house." The same accent.

Sitting up holding her head, suddenly remembering what happened, closing her eyes to block out the memory. "Where's your master gone?" said she on opening her eyes.

"He didn't say but was in a hurry. Have some wine." Taking a sip she felt the warmth going through her body.

Looking at the glass she murmured, "Ah! That's nice and strong." She held her head again.

Getting up and holding on to the chair, she looked around the room. *Nice,* she thought, *for a man alone.* Perhaps not alone. A noise outside drew her attention to the door.

The rider had a body over the saddle behind him. Milady let out a little cry, and putting a hand to her mouth, went towards the front door, still open, and looked up at Charles.

"He's dead. He was a bad'un. I'd warned him several times about his behaviour with women and ladies." It didn't make her feel any better.

"Just as well you had your pistol, the outcome could have been different. I am sorry if he's bothered you, he won't anymore."

"He worked for a smuggler," said she, looking at his face for a reaction.

A dark look came over his face but he showed no emotion. "Excuse me ma'am," letting his American accent slip, "I will just see to the body," and he went back out of the front door, then carried the lifeless body into the back room. Milady, overwhelmed with guilt, she wanted to go. She stopped holding her head, and looking at Agnes said, "Thank you for your kindness and tell your master..." She couldn't think of anything.

"Are you sure?"

"Yes, thank you." Walking to where her horse was tied, she wrapped her arms around his neck. "Come on boy, let's go home!" After checking the saddle she led him out of the stable. Putting her foot in the stirrup she mounted and trotted out of the courtyard, looking back at the big oak door and hoping for, she wasn't sure what. Turning on to the road she gently put her heels in the horse's side; he knew what she wanted him to do. The wind blowing though her hair, Star's mane blowing around, it was a moment of freedom. Reaching the beach path, she pulled the reins back.

"Whoa, boy!" stopping and looking out to sea, she smiled to herself, then, "This way, boy!" led him through a small gap in the bushes. Getting off her horse she tied him up where he could graze. She picked her skirts up and walked the short distance, looking around. There was no one in sight, and she stripped down to a petticoat. Walking towards the sea, the cool breeze caught the hairs on her arms. "I need this!" Picking the hem up she ran into the sea; the coldness took her breath away. She swam out to the rocks, going under the surface, the cold water washing over her body. Breathless! After a while she swam back, hoping the sea had washed both guilt and dirt away. She was refreshed, but the feeling was still there.

Walking out of the sea she was sobbing. Despite him being a bad man and doing bad things, she was suddenly overwhelmed by guilt. Going down on her knees she cried, "I killed a human being!" Looking down at the sea swirling around her knees she bent forward, and taking handfuls of water splashed her face, washing tears away. Getting up and walking towards Star she looked around, hoping no one saw her in her revealing state.

"Do you feel better for that?" Startled, she made no attempt to cover her body; if anything she felt excited as he enjoyed the view, looking her over in an obvious way. She walked ahead, picking up her clothes, taking her time putting them on. *Two can play games,* she thought.

"I came to find you to make sure you were all right." Looking into his handsome face she hadn't noticed before scars down one side, and down his neck and the portion of chest she could see.

Now she was dressed he came up close, put his hands around her waist, not taking his eyes off hers. She could feel his breath on her skin as he lifted her up on to Star as if she were a feather.

"Thank you Mr Long."

"I think Charles, as we've met. Don't you, Elizabeth?" She wanted to argue but the words wouldn't come out.

"Charles." She edged Star on with her knees and he obeyed. Looking back she could see he was still in the same spot, watching her.

Chapter Three

With the wind in her hair she felt like a young girl again. Cantering up to the gates she hoped they wouldn't notice any difference in her, after all she was still Lady Elizabeth Tremaine. Putting her chin up, she smiled to herself.

As if they knew she was approaching the front door opened, Dan came out and looked straight at her. "Milady, are you all right?" As he ran up to her, Star cantered up to Dan; he held Star as she dismounted.

"Is everyone here?"

"If you mean Ernest, yes, he's been looking for you," said Dan, glancing down so as to avoid eye contact.

"Oh!" Putting her chin up, she walked indoors. At the bottom of the staircase she was just about to quickly mount the stairs.

"Milady, did you have a pleasant swim?"

Looking around, "How did you know I had been swimming?" she exclaimed.

He said, laughing, "Your hair is wet!"

Touching her hair, "Oh yes," she said, smiling.

Ernest looked puzzled. "Is everything all right, Milady?" *He doesn't know,* she thought to herself, *no need for him to know now... well, unless I have to tell him.*

"We've got the chains on the fence," said she, looking back at him, "no need to worry about that unsavoury character, I shot him dead earlier." Ernest's mouth dropped open. He was about to speak when she picked her skirt up and walked up the stairs with as much decorum as she could muster. Ernest watched her go up. He gave a sigh. Trouble coming, he said to himself, out of earshot.

Milady felt annoyed with herself. Well, that didn't go according to plan, I am going to have to answer questions when I come back downstairs! Then she smiled to herself.

In her room, looking in the mirror, she saw her hair was a tangled mess. While she was brushing through the knots someone knocked.

"Yes, come in."

"Milady, do you need any help?"

"Yes please, you saw what a mess my hair was in," said she, laughing.

"Ernest sent me."

He doesn't miss a thing does he? Smiling at the young maid she turned around. "Let's see what we can do with my hair." Between them they made some sort order of her hair, brushed and tied to one side. Tabitha tied Milady's bodice up.

"Thank you, you can go now, I can finish dressing. I will be downstairs in a while. Where are the children?"

"Still in the conservatory playing, waiting to see you, Milady." She went out of the door.

One more look in the mirror. *What a day,* she thought.

Walking down the stairs she held the banister tightly. Ernest appeared at the bottom. "May I have a word, please?"

"Yes, but I must speak to the children first," said she, going into the warm conservatory.

"Mama!" Amelia ran to her. "Read to me."

"I will when you go to bed. Have you had tea yet?"

"Yes." She lifted the little girl up in her arms. "You smell of the sea!" She was smelling her mother's hair.

"I went for a swim in the sea."

"Can I go for a swim in the sea?"

"Oh no, far too cold for you and Charles!" She put the child down. "Come on now, bed time with Mattie. I have to speak to Ernest, then I will be up to read to you. You can choose your story or not."

"Margery book, please."

"Oh Goody Two-Shoes again! All right, up you go." She kissed them both as they went past. I must hide that cursed book, she murmured to herself.

She went into the big office. The 'tidy mice' had picked all the papers up and they were now neat on the desk. Ernest followed her in. "Milady," said he; walking right up to her he took her hand in his.

She looked down at his chafed thick-skinned hand; the owner had a soft heart. Looking into his face she said, "I left the cottages for home and I was set upon by that man we did business with earlier. He tried to get me off my horse. I warned him and the gun went off! I shot him in the chest; I wasn't aiming, it startled Star and he galloped off and I ended up at Mr Long's, Charles's house. I told him what happened. The man was his cousin, he said, he wasn't a nice man. Now he's a dead man!" Going to the brandy and pouring them both a drink she handed a glass to Ernest. "So there, that's what happened."

She sat down behind the desk. Before Ernest had a chance to say anything the door knocker went. Hugo appeared from somewhere, barking. The echo went around downstairs causing chaos. Ernest frowned as he went to the door. "Hugo, down!" He stopped barking but sat looking at the door, ready to pounce.

He opened the door to a neighbour. "Ah, Ernest!"

"Come in, sir." Ernest showed Mr Bennett into the parlour.

"How are you, Milady? I heard what happened today. Can I be of any assistance?" She held her hand out; his lips brushed her hand.

He was a friendly gentleman, himself widowed with grown-up children who lived at home with him. They all worked on the farm, except one son whom it was presumed died in America as he never returned home. It was never mentioned, being too painful for him, and of course there was Sophia who was in Paris, recovering from a broken heart.

"Would you like some brandy, Mr Bennett?"

"Robert! Please call me Robert. I think we have been neighbours long enough!"

Smiling back at him, "Yes, you're right," she said. "Please call me Elizabeth."

"So how are you?"

"I am fine. I was shocked, especially being attacked in daylight. My horse took me to Mr Long's cottage."

"There will be an informal inquest but nothing to worry about; I paid a visit to Mr Long and he informed me of his cousin attacking you. The authorities will not be taking it any further, as that is me! He also told me his cousin was an unsavoury sort, and that you were defending yourself."

Sitting down quickly she said, "It never occurred to me I might get into trouble."

"In other circumstances, it could be different, but with a respected man like Mr Long making a statement, and your intact reputation... We don't know if he was the highwayman."

Biting her lip, and with Ernest staring at her, she knew what he was thinking, not to mention she had shot someone before, possibly the highwayman.

Robert, oblivious to the tension between Ernest and Milady, carried on talking. "We are having a little soirée next Saturday; I will send an invitation." Getting up, "Must be off," he said, kissing her hand. "Be careful out there, you're a woman alone and these are dangerous times!"

"I have Ernest and the staff."

"Yes, yes of course." She knew what he meant. "Excellent brandy, by the way!"

"Yes it is."

He walked out of the parlour and was shown the front door by Ernest. She watched him get into his buggy; he was unable to get on a horse, now. Ernest came back in the room.

"What did he mean by that? Do you think he knows its origin?"

"No, he probably just liked it. A few gentlemen around here have contraband."

"Yes, but not all just killed a man."

"No, that's true!" said she, looking back at him in horror.

He laughed. "You're reading into a situation." She threw an apple at Ernest, catching it he took a bite. "You must control your temper!"

Sitting down she asked, "How much brandy do we have left from our secret source?"

"One bottle."

"The way I am drinking, it won't last long."

She drained her glass. "Good night, Ernest," said she, as she got up and walked towards the door. Stopping and turning around to look at Ernest, she added, "Be careful checking the house tonight."

"Night, Milady, I am about to do the last check."

"Be sure and take Hugo with you, I will be reading to Amelia if she is still awake."

Walking up the stairs and picking up a candle as she went, she listened to the noises in the house, Ernest talking to Hugo as they walked around the downstairs, Mrs West still pottering around in the kitchen, a gentle clatter of pots and plates, and now as she reached the top of the stairs, muffled voices behind the bedroom door. She walked in quietly. Charles was asleep, breathing gently, and Amelia was clutching her favourite book. Matilda got up. "Good night, Milady."

Smiling, she said, "See you in the morning, Matilda."

"So, where did we get to?" said she, taking the book from the little girl. Amelia was pointing to the page. "Poor Margery was very lonely indeed without her brother, and might have cried herself sick but for the new shoes that were brought home to her. They turned her thoughts from her grief, and as soon as she had put them on she ran in to Mrs Smith and cried out, "Two shoes, ma'am, two shoes!" Turning the page, her mother realised Amelia was closing her eyes. Sitting there for a few minutes to ensure she was asleep, Milady got off the bed and walked towards the curtains for a moment, feeling afraid at what she might see. She pulled one back and looking out at the sky a movement caught her eye. The peacocks were guarding the lawn, making a little noise. Then she saw him. She knew it was Charles on his horse, a shadow the other side of the fence. She touched her neck, down to the neckline of her dress. She moved back into the darkness to watch him unseen; *but he must have seen me,* she thought, as she pulled the curtains, resisting the urge to peep through.

Going to her room she met Hugo coming upstairs. "Hello, boy," said she, rubbing his head. He flopped down in his usual place, and she left the door open so she could hear the house. *He was dead, but there are others,* she thought as she nodded off in another night of restless sleep. Except this time it was disturbed by a nice man with smiling, dark eyes.

His hands around her waist, kissing her neck, nibbling her ears, "Elizabeth!" His lips worked their way down to her breasts! Oh! She awoke with a start, disappointed it was only a dream.

The house was still except for Hugo's snoring and the sound of two little children chattering and giggling.

Elizabeth stretched out her arms over her head, and then she remembered the previous day's events; shutting her eyes tight, she hoped the memory would go away; opening her eyes, she realised she was going to have to live with the memory, that she had killed another human being, a poor excuse for one but a human being nevertheless. And nothing she could do would change that.

"What's done is done," she said, throwing the covers back and going to the window, breathing in the cool dry air. Another lovely day. The curtains were blowing in a gentle breeze. The lawn did not look so menacing in the daylight; birds even risked landing to look for breakfast.

"Mama!" A smile crossed her face; she left her bedroom and went barefoot into the children's room. Both were awake and playing. Matilda was already up and sorting out clothes for the day.

"Have you any plans today, beg pardon Milady?"

"Can we go out, please?" The little girl looked up into her mother's eyes.

"Yes, we are taking the children down on to the beach."

Matilda looked horrified. "Do you think it is safe, Milady."

"Yes, there will be the three of us with the children, and the fresh air will do them good." Once the children were changed and fed, and instructions given to Mrs West for dinner, Ernest was told of their plan, much to his dismay.

The merry group, two children and three women, wandered down to the beach, the children holding Milady and Matilda's hands, and Tabitha in charge of the picnic basket. They found part of the beach was half-sheltered from the breeze by rocks.

A blanket was laid down on which Milady sat, watching the two women running around with the laughing children. She felt at ease, the first time in a couple of days. The gentle breeze kept the temperature down.

"This way, Charles!" she called as he tried to kick a ball; he fell on his knees, getting up quickly. "There's a brave boy!" she said, rubbing his knees though the thin cloth. Tears averted, he ran after his sister.

Milady wandered down to the water's edge, looking out to sea, her bonnet tied on but still having put her hair up to save it. A ship in the distance was bobbing up and down in the waves.

"Mama!" Turning around quickly for a second, she had forgotten the recent events.

"Yes!" Turning she ran up to the little boy, kicking the ball towards him.

A peaceful couple of hours were spent in the glorious sunshine. Sitting down on the blanket under a parasol the children ate bread and butter with cheese, and a piece of cake and an apple. "We will have to carry you back after all that," said Milady, looking at the food, "and if we drink too much mead we won't get back!"

The women were laughing. Taking her hat off she said, "Ahh, that's better!" Her hair was blowing around her face.

"Milady, you'll have trouble brushing your hair again," said Tabitha, laughing.

"But yes, Tabitha, you do such a good job!"

Tabitha giggled.

"How is your young man?"

"Jonas is fine." Tabitha was looking all coy.

"He works for Mr Bennett, doesn't he?" said Milady, trying to keep last night's meeting out of her head, "he is a nice man, and I am sure a fair one."

Then she looked at Matilda. "When are you and Ernest getting married? Is there any date set yet?"

Looking embarrassed, "We were hoping before Christmas," said she.

"We will have to see what we can do." Returning to her book with one eye on the children, and having to squint through the sun's rays, she put her hat on, lowered over her eyes.

A horse in the distance was approaching them fast. "Milady!" A frightened Tabitha didn't know whether to grab the children and run, or to hide. Matilda was looking around for a stick.

Milady got up, her hat falling off. She put her hand up to shield her eyes from the sun. "It is all right, it's Mr Long, although I don't think he has seen us. We are sheltered here; he *is* in a hurry!"

As he got nearer he slowed down, a movement caught his eye; he didn't expect to see the little group by the rocks.

Her heart raced, there were butterflies in the pit of her stomach and she felt flushed. *Idiot, it was only a dream,* she thought to herself, *he wasn't really there.*

"That's a fine-looking horse there, muscular... umm... The rider's not bad, either!" Milady and Tabitha were looking now at Matilda, who realising she had spoken out loud, exclaimed, "Ooh, pardon me, Milady!"

The women were laughing as he trotted up to them. "Ladies, a lovely day for it!"

As he got down off the horse Amelia walked up to him. "Hello, my name is Amelia," she said, then turning around to look at Charles, "and this is my brother Charles." She touched the horse's nose; it swished its tail quite happily, standing there being admired by this little human creature.

"I am older than Charles. Mama said he is the baby."

Smiling at her daughter as Amelia walked back to the two women, who were trying not to stare, Milady said, "Thank you for speaking to the magistrate." She looked down at her hands.

"It's the least I could do. I told the magistrate before gossip got there first. I should not have allowed him to wander around." He looked to be in deep thought. "How are you, Elizabeth?" said he, catching hold of her hands.

"It has been a turbulent couple of days, with the highwayman as well. But I am fine. Thank you for enquiring."

"There is no sign of the highwayman. Perhaps he is resting." *He doesn't know I shot him,* she thought. She looked straight into his face. "Yes, perhaps he is."

Going into his pocket he said, "Your pistol, Milady."

"I'd forgotten about it."

"Were you not lost without it?" A smile crossed his face.

"I have not felt a need to carry a pistol since..." trailing off, not wanting to say it out loud.

"I have cleaned it for you." He held the pistol in both hands as if it were heavy, staring down at the offending object that saved her life.

"Thank you, sir."

"I must be off." Taking her hand he kissed it while still looking into her eyes. She felt a sensation she had not felt for years, if ever. Turning, putting his foot in the stirrup and mounting his horse, he galloped away towards his destination, that only he knew. *I wonder where he's going, and along the beach and not the path,* she thought.

The sun had moved around the rocks; they were in the shade and the children were shivering, despite running around.

"Right, children, time to go home!" Moaning but doing as they were asked, they put their shoes on, then the tired group wandered back to the house.

Hugo ran out to meet them, running around like a puppy. "Hugo, come on boy, you can come next time!"

They patted his head and he calmed down. He walked towards the house with them until he heard a rustle in the bushes; then off he sprung, coming back looking slightly bedraggled. Later, after the children were in bed and Milady had read Goody Two-Shoes again, she was in the conservatory reading a book with a brandy in her hand, trying to concentrate. She went to the French window; the moon was full, casting a shadow over the lawn. A shiver went down her back. Making sure the doors were shut, she picked the candle up leaving her book on the desk, picked up her glass in the other hand and headed towards the kitchen. Cook had gone to bed. Placing the glass on the table she poured herself some milk then turned and walked towards the stairs.

Hearing voices outside, she blew the candle out. Ernest was outside talking to someone. Straining her ears she heard Charles's voice; *he was talking to Charles, I wonder why,* she thought. Hearing the door go, she carefully tiptoed up the rest of the stairs and went to her bedroom, picking up a lit candle on the way across to the window. I won't hide, this is my house! She pulled the curtains back just in time to see a big brown horse go out by the drive, and as though he knew he was being watched, he turned around, stopped, looked straight at her window and left.

Chapter Four

Coming down the stairs, she called, "Morning Ernest." Looking at his back she went straight in for the kill. "Why was Charles here last night?"

Avoiding her face, occupying himself with his boots at the bottom of the stairs, he replied, "He came to make sure all was well."

"Ahh! Did you get some more brandy from him?"

He looked up at her. "How did you know?"

"Well, his cousin collected the money, so I guessed, and your face said it all. When are the goods coming?"

"Tonight."

"And where are you meeting him?"

"In the barn."

"Well, I will meet him!"

"Milady!" She was now at the bottom of the stairs, looking straight into Ernest's face.

"He won't harm me."

She was curious as to what he would say when he saw her. Was it the risk that made her excited, or was it the rendezvous at night alone with that handsome man? And why was he occupying her dreams at night?

The day was dry and muggy, everyone was busy. Tabitha was hanging washing out, Matilda was washing the children in the warm conservatory, Dan was sweeping out the barn, Ernest was at the cottages helping with the repairs and Milady was sorting out the paper work, bills paid and the ones awaiting payment. She sat back in the chair. *So, to town tomorrow to pay this lot... but that's tomorrow,* she thought to herself.

Picking her bonnet up and walking out through the study door she passed Tabitha in the hallway. She was rolling rugs up to brush outside while it was dry. "I am going to the beach if anyone is looking for me. I won't be long," said Milady.

Looking at Milady as she passed, Tabitha said, "Oh, all right, I will tell Matilda!" Milady fastened her bonnet.

With hair flowing she walked across the lawn, reaching the path to the beach. "The tide's in…good, I won't have to walk so far," she murmured.

Stripping down to her petticoat she looked around, there was no one in sight. She tied her hair in a plait. "There'll be no knots this time!" The water was cold but refreshing, though the petticoat was a hindrance. Looking around, and still on her own, she stood and slipped it over her head, and threw it onto the shore.

"That's better!" Turning around and swimming out, she dived under, touching the sand. Coming back up and suddenly realising she was vulnerable, she made her way back to shore. She crouched down, looking around, there was no sign of anyone. Standing up and still looking around, she quickly walked to pick up her petticoat, and slipping it over her head, put the rest of her clothes on.

She had done this since she was a child, against her parents' wishes. "Most unbecoming of a young lady!" they would say, but to no avail; she was a tomboy, more so than some boys.

"Where does she get this wildness from?" she once heard her mother ask her father. He would just smile.

"She'll grow out of it, my love." But she never did.

"Just as well, my mama can't see me like this!" said she, looking down at the wetness coming through her dress exposing cold nipples, and smiling to herself.

Crossing the lawn she saw Ernest coming through the gate. She waved; he waving back wearily made his way towards her. "We have done well today; half of us did the roofs, the rest on the fields. Oh, Lottie's about to have her baby, she's been trying all night, according to Matthew!"

"I'll ride over to see if I can help," said she, tripping towards the stable. "Dan, can you saddle Star please? And good, the weather is holding," she added, looking up at the sky, as if she could foretell the weather for the next couple of days.

"Just a few more days and all will be done with the cottages."

"So we are waiting on the pilchards?" A question and a statement, looking in earnest at Ernest.

"Yes, cellar and salt ready, just waiting for them to swim this way," said he smiling, "with help of course!"

"When are the boats going out?"

"The lookouts will tell us when they see them off shore."

Walking indoors she was greeted by two little children running around with Matilda trailing after them and looking tired.

She felt sorry for the older woman. "I won't be long. Have the afternoon off when I come back."

"Ooh Milady, thank you!"

Riding out of the gate, the wind blowing her hair behind her, she arrived in time to hear a baby crying. "It's a boy!" shouted a happy Matt.

"How's Lottie?"

"Tired, but well, thank ee, Milady."

She looked into the little squashed face. "Ooh, you had trouble, didn't you! Can I see Lottie?"

"Yes, of course!" he said, leading the way into the dimly lit cottage. It was warm, especially with its repaired roof. "Lottie, Milady is here!"

A tired-looking woman looked up. Elizabeth's heart went out to her. "You're young and strong, you'll soon be back on your feet." After a short while Milady was on the way back to relieve a tired Matilda and she was gone, no delaying. Milady smiled to herself; she knew Ernest had finished work so they would have some time together. She settled down to play with the excitable children. Amelia had her baby doll and Charles had a wooden cart, Finding a book other than Goody Two-Shoes, she said, "Let's read, Amelia, in English, then we will do some French." She looked up at the large clock on the mantelpiece; *only two o'clock,* she thought, *time is dragging.* She sat with her back to the clock so she would not watch it. Reading was done; Amelia was a quick learner.

"Good girl, our one little sentence today in French."

"*Je m'appelle* Amelia, *je suis âgée de quatre ans.*"

"*Ma bonne fille!*"

Charles was fidgety, "I'm hungry!"

She looked at the clock, it was nearly four. "Come on then, down to the kitchen, let's see what Mrs West has made." She held their hands, and they walked across the hallway to the corridor which opened into the back parlour.

The two children ran to their chairs. Milady walked in behind them and helped Charles up onto his chair. Then she cut up his meat and potatoes.

"Milady, would you like yours now?"

"Yes please, I think I will," said she, smiling down at her children.

Ernest and Matilda came in. "Food smells good!"

"Sit down then and I'll dish ee up some." They did as they were told, and Mrs West sat down as well.

"Where's Tabitha?" asked Milady.

"Seeing her young man!"

Bang, bang! There was a heavy knock on the old front door. Ernest and Hugo jumped up, Hugo barked and Charles started crying. "There, there!" Milady picked him up and gave him to Mattie as she ran after Ernest and Hugo, picking her gun up which was no good as it was unloaded.

Another knock at the door. "Hold on there, sir!" Ernest unlocked the door to several men in red.

"Sorry to bother you, sir," said one, nodding to Milady, "Madam, we are looking for smugglers, they were on the beach and as you're the closest house…"

Milady had now caught her breath, holding the pistol behind her back. "We are having dinner, Captain, and we have not seen any strangers around here, only you and your men!"

Not liking the answer but having to accept it, "Thank you," he said, nodding his head. "Come on, men."

And they were gone. Ernest and Milady looked at each other. "Are they looking for him?"

"I don't know. Probably him and his men."

"Do you know when the boat came in?"

Talking quietly he said, "In the last couple of days. They seem to move it on quickly."

She was getting her coat on. "Where are you going?"

"Get your coat, Ernest, please! I think I know where he is."

"Where?"

Looking wild-eyed, she said, "The beach, the labyrinthine caves."

Thinking for a second, then putting his coat on and grabbing his pistol, he said, "Some of his men won't know us... Is yours loaded?"

"No, doing it now."

Turning around, Ernest had a serious expression on his face. "And, don't shoot anything in red... You'll hang!"

Speaking to Matilda she said, "Put the children to bed please. See you all in a while," she added, taking a minute to look back at her little family.

"I do not shoot everything that moves..."

"No, but when you do shoot, you hit your target!"

"Yes," said she smiling, "I suppose I do."

They crept across the lawn, still daylight but fading fast; the area was strangely quiet. Milady crouched down behind a large hydrangea bush, Ernest right beside her. "The army were riding away towards the next beach where Charles could have been heading earlier. This way!" Ernest pointed to a gap in the bushes. They pushed their way through the gap looking around as they went. There was shooting and shouting on the other beach. Ernest pulled her down in the sand dunes. "Down here, quick!" There were riders and men running; a couple were shot in the back but most escaped.

She squinted. "That's him, the rider on the brown horse, he looks injured!"

Grabbing her arm he whispered, "Let's go back, we can't do anything here." Reluctantly she agreed, and they retraced their steps onto the lawn, walking quickly to the back of the house, into the kitchen and making them all jump.

"Sorry," looking at the nervous women and children unaware, "we were too late. The military got them first."

"There are gentlemen in the front parlour, I am making them a drink."

"Oh! Who is it?"

"Mr Bennett and a Mr Carnot."

Brushing her hair back off her face and taking her coat off, she said, "Where did you say I was? And who is Mr Carnot?"

"Visiting the cottages, Milady, I couldn't think what else to say."

"No, that's good."

"And I do not know Mr Carnot."

She went towards the front parlour with Mrs West behind her. "Good evening, gentlemen!" They both stood and nodded. "Please be seated," she said as Mrs West served them tea.

"We heard you were visiting your cottages! May I introduce a friend from London, Mr Carnot." He stood up again and took her hand. *Soft hands! I wonder what he does for a living,* she thought.

"Yes, but I heard shooting, so I came back."

"Very wise, not safe out there. I understand there are smugglers around."

"I don't think it is the smugglers shooting." Changing the subject rapidly, she asked, "So how are you, Robert?"

"Wonderful, Elizabeth! I have your invitation for my little soiree on Saturday."

"I hope to claim a dance, Milady!" said Mr Carnot, smiling at Elizabeth in a mysterious manner. She couldn't understand his airs or gestures.

"Elizabeth, please call me Elizabeth."

"And call me Lazare, I am French, I always explain as people do ask." He made a very elaborate bow. She looked at him, puzzled.

Later, reading the invitation, *I wonder if Charles will go,* she thought, looking out of the window. It was dark enough now. Finding a thin shawl and putting it over her shoulders she made her way down the stairs, hoping no one would see her. Taking an oil lamp turned low she made her way to the barn. It was Dan's night off, so no one should be around. Raising the latch disturbed the horses. "*Ssh!*" said she, patting their heads.

"Over here!" It startled her! She turned around. He was behind the door, he closed it as she entered the barn. He was feeling irritable, the military had nearly got them. His mood lightened on seeing Elizabeth. "Why are you here? Where's Ernest?"

"I wanted to meet you, um, to see if you were all right…"

"We heard the shooting."

Her heart was ready to burst. A crooked smile crossed his face. He was beside her, putting his arm around her waist; she lifted her chin, wanting to be kissed. He obliged, now wrapping both arms around her tightly. He winced slightly, only coming up for air; he surprising himself that he enjoyed it so much. They kissed again, his kisses trailed down her neck, opening up her dress to find her heaving breasts. His tongue tasted her skin. It was salty. A pair of eyes caught the encounter, the owner turned away and went back in the house. Ernest frowned, "More trouble!"

Finding his belt then undoing it, she could feel he was enjoying the moment as much as she. "Ooh!" He took an intake of breath as she touched him. He lifted her skirts up as he laid her down on the straw. She gasped. He stopped, looking into her eyes.

"It's all right… Just been a while…"

When they were both satisfied he helped her up, and she brushed her clothes down. "Were you injured earlier?" she enquired, looking at the blood on his shirt as she pulled her stays together, tying a bow at her breasts.

"Only my arm, bullet went through." Making conversation seemed strange. Looking at her, *I don't need any complications,* he thought, *this could be trouble.* He regained his composure.

"I have put your goods under the hay in the first stable, Ernest knows about the arrangement for payment."

"I will get Ernest to move it."

He hesitated, leant forward, kissed her cheek and was gone. She did not know how she felt but she enjoyed the encounter and wanted more. Making sure she had no straw in her hair she looked outside the barn, turned the lamp out and walked to the back of the house, creeping in and locking the door. "Is everything all right?"

"Ernest, you made me jump!"

"Yes," he said.

"You know about payment. It is in the first stable, under the straw. Good night, Ernest." Walking out she didn't want him to look into her face because he would know. Hugo came to meet her, looking at her suspiciously. "I have been in the barn with the horses," she murmured, patting his head. Hugo as usual flopped down outside her room and she pushed her door to. Finally undressed, in her flimsy nightgown, she pulled her curtains back. The sea was crashing on the shore; she could smell the sea air. She touched her neck, then down to her breasts. She saw him on his brown horse on the other side of the fence as he rode off. She suddenly felt lonely and wanted his arms around her. *Stop it,* she said to herself.

She slept well, no unfinished dreams.

Awake, stretching, she covered her face. "Did I really do that? I intend to do it again!"

But today it was off to town. She dressed plainly, hair tied to one side.

"Good morning," said she, looking around at the little gathering in the kitchen. "Ernest, are you busy this morning? I need to go to town. I would like some company, please."

He was looking at her, puzzled. "Yes, I can do the fences later."

The weather had turned cold; a strong wind was coming in off the sea. "I think summer is nearly over," said she, feeling sad; she liked swimming in the sea; she could do so still, but it was not so pleasurable.

"So why the need for my company? It is not like you!"

"I know. The last time I went into town I met the highwayman. I don't want to risk it again. I was lucky last time."

Mounting their horses they rode out of the drive. "Have you much money about you?"

"A little. If it is not enough, I can visit the bank, although I wish not to."

The journey was uneventful. "Perhaps the change in the weather has kept the bad men in," said she, looking at Ernest and laughing.

"More like blood poisoning from a bullet!"

Riding along the path with the bushes overgrown was making it a damp experience. They chatted, but all the time stayed alert. They reached Polperro. The sea was lapping against the seawall, the little boats bobbing up and down. "Are you all right on your own? I have some business to conduct," said Ernest, looking serious.

The fishermen were on their way out to sea while the tide was high; it was a hive of activity. "Looks busy today. Oh, the circus is here! And yes, I will be fine."

Hustle and bustle; painted people walking around, children skipping and following the clown, the man with a lighted stick, putting it down his throat just to extinguish the flame, making the children scream with delight.

Milady smiled at Ernest. "I am going to pay some bills," said she, raising her eyebrows. *I wonder where he is off to,* she thought as she watched Ernest walk away, hands in his pockets, looking at ease but still looking around.

She called after him. "Shall we meet in 'The Three Pilchards'? I'll get us a meal." He waved in acknowledgement. So to business. The little shop next to the bank caught her attention. Hats and lace! So pretty! A bit of lace won't be too extravagant, she tried to persuade herself. I have so many dresses, a bit of lace will liven up an old one.

She chose a cream frilly lace. "An excellent choice, Milady!" There was a jolly mood all around; even the soldiers looked happy.

She replied with a "Good morning!" as she left the little shop.

Bills paid, now a look around. Then she saw him; a lean, muscular figure, his long coat billowing out behind him, his tricorne hat firmly in place. He saw her while making his way through the crowd and he nodded. "Milady!" Keeping a respectable distance both resisted the urge to lunge at each other. Her insides did a little flip, thinking to herself, *I feel like a young girl!* "Have you finished your business here?"

"No, I am meeting Ernest."

"About yesterday..." He was looking for the right words! "I didn't mean for that to happen."

She felt disappointed; he leaned forward and whispered, "But I am glad it did!" Now she felt elated.

"Can we meet later? Come to my house; Agnes will be there but she'll pay no heed."

"At what time?"

"Any time. I am on the way back now," he nodded. "Milady."

Her insides flipped. Oh where we are going with this? He is not the marrying sort! "Umm," said she, turning around, "Ernest, have you finished your business?"

"Yes, so now some food."

The tavern was busy, cards being won and lost, voices raised! They walked through to the lounge and found a little table by the window. The landlady came over, a buxom woman, very heavy-breasted, wiping her hands on her less than clean apron.

"Sir, madam; what canna get thee?"

"Mutton and bread with two mugs of ale, please.

Ernest looked at Milady. "I can eat anything, you know that!" said she.

"Yes, but this is not a good place for a lady to be seen."

"When have I been a proper lady?"

"Yes, well, when you put it like that… And I know I am your servant, but be careful with Mr Long, please. Now you can tell me off for my insolence!" He looked down at his drink that had been slammed down in front of him.

She touched his hand. "Ernest, you are my best friend! Everything you do is for my good, even if I don't appreciate it at the time. I know what I am doing with Charles, I hope, so let's drink up. Good health!" said she, holding up her mug.

Ernest looked into her face. "And yours too, Milady!" Their pewter mugs chinked.

Looking out of the window she said, "Do you like a circus, Ernest?"

"No, it brings unsavoury characters into the village."

"At least the smugglers get a rest." Hearing a noise outside, she added, "Except the soldiers are here in great force!"

"Oh I see where you're going with this, there's no cargo coming in the near future," said Ernest with the lie all over his face.

"That meal tasted better than it looked!" Ernest belched.

They finished up their ale. "Goodness, that was strong," said Milady, "I'd better hang onto Star." Composure regained they went outside, it was time to go home. Taking a careful walk to the stables they looked around; people were smiling, children laughing; it had to be good if only for a short while! The excitement was contagious.

The horses were rested. Ernest and the stablehand saddled the horses; they mounted and were on their way.

"What are you doing this afternoon, Ernest?"

"Looking over the vegetables and the garden, generally mucking in, Milady."

"You'd better check the hen house. It's going to be a hard winter for the wild life as well; they might look for easy pickings.'

"And you, Milady?"

"I am visiting our neighbour. I want to see if he has been invited on Saturday."

They rode on in silence, listening to the birds and the sea crashing in. The alcohol had a slight effect on Milady; she was quiet, thinking deeply.

A dog was barking, distant voices could heard out to sea, and there were fishing boats just off shore. A cool breeze caught her hair. "At least it is dry…" With that it started to rain.

Both were laughing. "My fault!" said she, as she put her hood over her hair.

"Race you back!" Ernest shot off. Elizabeth was startled but soon recovered; she caught up, just as he got into the yard before her. "I won!" said he, laughing despite the rain.

"You won because you're wearing britches!"

"No, because I am a better rider then you!" She stood up in her stirrups, leant over and slapped Ernest on the arm."

"I still won."

"Next time."

They cantered towards the stable. All was quiet, and Dan could be heard making horseshoes.

"I will take the horses, Milady."

Dismounting and rushing indoors, she could not get any more drenched. She was standing in the doorway. *I cannot visit today, he will understand,* she thought to herself.

Walking to the conservatory, she paused in the doorway. "Hello darlings!"

"Mama!"

"Have you been good for Matilda?"

"Yes," they said, but looking guilty.

"I'll change into dry clothes and join you." She went upstairs and having changed out of her wet clothes, she came down and played and read with the children. It was a quiet afternoon.

The rain continued to lash at the windows; *they did the roofs in time,* she thought to herself.

The big table was set for dinner in the dining room. Sitting at the table Milady and Matilda both kept an eye on the children.

There was a knock on the old oak door, Ernest answered it coming back into the dining room. "Milady, it is Mr Long to see you." Milady got up and met Charles at the dining room door.

"I came to ensure you were safe, as I did not see you today!"

"As you see I am perfectly safe! I just got drenched on the way home. Join us, we have plenty."

"Yes, please, I will," said he, giving his hat and coat to Ernest.

"Ernest, will you ask Mrs West for another place setting, please."

The evening was pleasant. Oil lamps were lit and the fire was blazing. Matilda took the children to bed with a promise to read later, or in the morning if they were asleep.

They took brandy in the study. "A fine tipple, this!" she said, raising her glass.

He laughed. "Yes, it is!"

"Are you going on Saturday to Mr Bennett's dance?"

"Yes I am."

"Well, I shall see you there."

"I would like to see you before then."

Her body knew what he meant. "Tomorrow I might just be out and about, riding Star... I might even pass your way," said she, smiling. He got up, then taking the last sip, he put his glass down. "I shall look forward to accidentally meeting you tomorrow." She saw him to the door. He turned around and bent forward, taking her hand in his and kissing it gently, keeping his eyes on her face. "Tomorrow, then."

She watched him go out through the front door, and on hearing his horse galloping away she lifted the lamp and went into the study to check the French windows. She saw Ernest in the hallway.

"All checked, Milady. I will walk around with Hugo."

"Thank you, good night Ernest!"

I shall never sleep tonight smiling to herself... as she swept upstairs with candle in one hand and her dress hem in the other.

Chapter Five

The house creaked as it settled into a peaceful night. The children had long gone to sleep. Using the light from the candle stub to find her way around their untidy room, Milady touched their heads, feeling melancholic. *I'll read to them in the morning,* she thought, going towards the window and pulling the curtains back. The sea looked rough, the sky clear, the stars out, and the moon causing the peacocks to cast shadows on the lawn. And a hive of wild animal activity in the bushes preventing a quiet night for the peacocks who were strutting around.

Leaving their room she stepped over Hugo who looked up but didn't move. "'Night, boy!"

She settled into a dream-filled sleep... dark eyes and those hands all over her body...

"Mama?"

"Ooh, morning Charles," said she, stretching. "I am awake, I am awake."

"Read, please!"

"Sorry, Milady, Master Charles got away from me.' Breathlessly the woman bustled into the room.

"That's all right, Matilda."

"Come on, Master Charles, let's get you dressed," said she, taking Charles by the hand and continuing to scold him for running into Mama's room so early.

Climbing out of bed, stretching and shivering, with bare feet she padded over the worn mat to the little bowl on the table. She poured out some water. "Ooh, it's colder this morning!" After washing in the little bowl she quickly dressed, lacing up her bodice, and putting a little rose water between her breasts. She smiled to herself.

During breakfast with the children she said, "When you've finished your porridge we'll read 'Cinderella'."

Amelia made a face. "But Mama!"

"We have not read this one." Later, a couple of chapters read, the two children were bored with Cinderella, and getting tetchy. Getting up and brushing her dress down, she said, "Well, I am going out for a couple of hours, children. Be good for Matilda," she added, kissing the tops of their heads. She found Ernest in the hallway.

"Ernest, I am calling on Mr Long." She fiddled with her scarf, trying not to smile or to look directly at him. Equally she didn't see the look of concern in his face; when she turned around Ernest smiled.

"It looks dry today, but be careful Milady." Oh, as an afterthought, "Are you carrying your pistol?"

"Yes," said she, patting her side.

Dan saddled Star. Mounting and sitting astride the placid horse she cantered out of the gate, taking a deep breath and sniffing the fresh air; a good day to be alive. Money was tucked away in her bag and she gave a reassuring pat on Star's neck.

Birds were singing and flying around the trees that swayed with the gentle sea breeze, the sea relentlessly crashing in over the sand. Star clip-clopped along the dry, once muddy path, his hoofs making a little noise, as Milady looked around, trying not to let her imagination get the better of her. She felt relieved when she reached Mr Long's house; she wanted to gallop in, but with her chin up, looking every part the lady, Star trotted into the courtyard. Charles was outside, brushing down his beautiful brown horse. Both creatures stood proud. Charles stopped and looked at the approaching visitor. He spoke to his groom, then walking towards her his crooked smile crossed his face.

"Morning, Elizabeth!"

"Morning, Charles." She was admiring his firm body, his biceps bulging though his shirt. A little sweat was trickling down his face. He saw she had noticed, and he wiped his face with his shirt sleeve, making him look even more attractive.

Now Star was standing in front of him shaking his mane. Gently, Charles put his hands up around her waist. She looked into his eyes, allowing him to lift her down slowly; she swung her leg over Star's head, and sliding down the length of Charles's firm, sweaty body, her insides did a little flutter. Her eyes didn't leave his face. Breaking the silence in a husky voice Charles cleared his throat. "This way," said he, taking her gloved hand in his and kissing it. *Ooh, be still my heart, I hope I am not blushing,* Elizabeth thought as she took a sly glance at his profile. Almost caught, she quickly came back to the moment.

"Would you like a drink?" Agnes appeared from somewhere.

Looking towards Agnes she said, "Tea, please." Charles looked surprised.

"Not wine?"

"A little early for me!" And I want my wits about me...

"A tray of tea, please Agnes."

Once Agnes had left the room, she reached into her bag and handed him the little bundle. "Thank you."

He hesitated, then getting up from the chair he put the bundle in the safe behind a painting of a half-naked woman from the Renaissance period, languishing on a chaise longue.

Running her fingers over the piano keys, she said, "Do you play?"

"No."

"So why have a piano?" said she, running her fingers again over the keys, but resisting the urge to sit and play. "I like to play, I haven't done for so long," she said quietly, thinking of long ago when her governess taught her.

"So that beautiful women will play for me."

Coming back to the moment. "Does it work?"

"Well, you just did," said he, smiling.

"I just tickled the keys."

They drank their tea, making polite conversation. Charles got up, took Elizabeth's hand and looking into her eyes, he saw desire that matched his...

"This way!" Kissing her now gloveless hand, he led her up the stairs.

She felt embarrassed. "Won't Agnes wonder where we have gone?"

Laughing, he said, "She might, but she knows her place, and keeps her own counsel whilst in my house; she has worked for me a long time."

Opening a door and letting her enter, he shut it behind them. He came up behind her, putting his arms around her waist, kissing her ear and neck, his warm breath making her shudder. She undid her blouse, slowly turning around to look at him. Loosening her bodice his hands now explored her body, kissing her neck. She groaned. They proceeded to undress each other with giggling nervousness and impatience. Finally, down to skin, they delighted each other gently, then passionately.

Later, lying in each other's arms, she asked, "Do you dance?" He was looking at her, puzzled.

"Yes, but I fear not your polite English type of dancing! And why?"

"I will have to teach you for Mr Bennett's ball on Saturday," she said, "although I fear it is so soon we do not have time for a lesson." Lying in his arms and running her fingers over a deep scar on his chest, she wanted to ask so many questions in her head, but nothing came out of her mouth; perhaps because she didn't want to ruin the moment.

"You can teach me anything you wish, Elizabeth," said he as he covered her mouth with his. They continued to please each other late into the afternoon.

She was riding back to her home, deep in thought.

"Good day to you, Milady!"

She was startled. "Captain Edwards!"

"You shouldn't be out alone, we still have not apprehended the highwayman. He seems to have well

disappeared, my men and I cannot find any trace of him!"
Keep calm, he doesn't know, she thought.

"I had forgotten about that scoundrel." She was lying.
"Where do you think he is?"

"I think he either came to harm or is recovering from
something."

Riding beside Elizabeth he accompanied her home. She
found his company enjoyable, but was careful not to let her
guard down, so she was not as relaxed as she would have
liked to be. Growing up she was a terrible liar, her dearest
father could see right through her every lie; she found it
easier in the long run just to own up. Looking at Captain
Edwards as he talked, she caught the tail end of the
conversation he apparently was having with himself as she
was paying no attention.

"So the army will be here a while."

"Umm, I beg your pardon, I missed that!"

"Due to the circus and the recent smuggling activities,
and the shooting of course, we will be here a while to assist
the militia."

"Well, for whatever reason, it will be nice to have the
company of the military, some reassurance in these troubling
times. Would you like some refreshment, Captain
Edwards?" said she as they arrived at the wrought iron gates.

"Thank you but alas, I must be on my way, duty calls."
He nodded and was gone.

Trotting towards the stable she called, "Hallo Dan."
Dismounting, she gave the reins to Dan, who took Star into
the stable.

"Thank you. Oh, Dan, can you check Star's hoofs please,
one sounded a bit hollow."

"Yes Milady."

Walking through the house the smell of food filled her
nostrils. Everyone except Matilda and the children were in
the kitchen. Ernest stood up. "Milady."

"It's all right, Ernest." She signalled for him to sit back
down; happy with this he did so. "Where are the children?"

"Having a bath, they got rather dirty in the garden!"

Smiling and looking towards the conservatory, "In the conservatory?" she enquired.

"Yes, we didn't want to trail mud though the house."

"Mud! What they have been up to?" Looking back at Ernest as she went to leave the kitchen, she stopped and spoke in a nonchalant manner.

"Oh Ernest! Captain Edwards escorted me home along the beach path. The highwayman hasn't been seen again, he doesn't know why!"

She said this looking directly into Ernest's eyes. Hugo came bounding in after her. "Hello boy!" She patted his head.

Walking with him she found the children sitting together in the little tin bath; Matilda was washing their hair. "Milady." Matilda was bending down on her knees.

"Have you been good?"

Both children looked at Matilda. "Yes, Mama." She looked at Matilda who smiled and shrugged one shoulder. "Umm!" The children looked sheepish. "Have we been a little naughty?"

Before she could finish, "It was Charles!" said Amelia. Milady, surprised at the child's outburst, looked at her daughter. "He did it, Mama!"

"He is only two and a half! You on the other hand, are nearly five!" said she, trying to stifle a smile. She looked at Matilda. "What happened?"

"The flowers that were still in the garden, were, um, picked. It's a mess out there, I only turned away for a minute; it will take Ernest a while to tidy the ground." Matilda looked towards the very large vase filled with a range of flowers in all colours.

Tilting her head to one side, "Well, it's pretty, I suppose!" said Milady, trying not to smile.

"I think tomorrow both of you will help Ernest in the garden." This was not really a punishment as they liked being in the garden.

Later, when all were sitting at the large kitchen table, "Well, Ernest, they are with you tomorrow," said Milady. Ernest was keeping a straight face.

"I'll work them hard, Milady!"

The two little faces looked up, bottom lips quivering. "After your tea we will read, when you are tucked up in bed."

Later still in the kitchen all were around the table except Dan who was still in the barn.

"How was Mr Long?" asked Ernest, looking up from taking a mouthful of delicious smelling food.

Half looking at Ernest she said, "He was fine, he is going on Saturday but he does not dance."

"Plenty of other things for him to occupy himself with, especially if he's a gambling man, and I have a feeling he is," said he, looking at his squirming mistress, who was trying hard not to look into Ernest's face.

"Mrs West, I have not sewn for a while. Can you help me sew some lace on my green dress, please? It'll liven it up, don't you think? I do not need any more dresses."

"Yes, of course Milady, let me know when you're ready in the morning."

Looking at her plate of food, "Captain Edwards said the highwayman could still be nearby," she said, "but he hasn't been seen for a while, so his whereabouts is unknown. Where would someone like him hide unseen?" Unspoken messages passed between them.

"There's some talk of an unknown man living rough in the woods," said Ernest.

The mood became solemn, everyone was in their own thoughts, even the children were quiet. "Will he get us, Mama?" Two little faces were looking up from their food.

"No, my darlings!"

Later, Milady was upstairs, sitting on one of the children's beds.

"Once upon a time, there was a wealthy widower who married a proud and haughty woman as his second wife. She had two daughters, who were equally vain and selfish. By his first wife he'd had a beautiful young daughter, a girl of unparalleled goodness and sweet temper. The stepmother and her daughters forced the first daughter into servitude where she was forced to work day and night, doing menial chores..."

The children were now asleep tucked up in bed. *They must be tired,* she thought to herself. I read this chapter this morning and they didn't moan, or didn't realise.

Climbing into bed, she felt a tremor of excitement when she thought of Saturday night. "But my dress first!" she said to herself.

It seemed as though she had just closed her eyes when the sun came peering in the partially open curtains, and never one to stay in bed when the sun was up, she swung her legs over the edge. She could hear the house was already awake. "Do they ever sleep?" she asked herself.

A loud knock came at the door. "Hevva! Hevva!" someone shouted below stairs.

"Pilchards are here, Milady!"

"Yes, Ernest, I heard, I am coming!" Finding old clothes and boots she ran down the stairs to see Ernest, Dan and Hugo waiting for her. She gave instructions to the women. "Garden later, play with them indoors, please." She hesitated, as though she was going to add something.

"Yes, Milady," answered Tabitha.

Changing her mind, "See you later," said she, as she hastily put on her boots. Dan had saddled the horses and all three rode off, the messenger sharing Dan's horse.

Reaching the cliff overlooking the cove, they saw the little boats with their nets were dragging the unsuspecting pilchards towards the waiting fishermen and families. There was laughter and chatter. "Winter might not be so harsh after all," said Ernest.

"We won't starve anyway." The women and children sat on the rocks, putting the fish in barrels of salt. "Quite a catch."

"Yes, and enough to sell to Italy; I think a little celebration tonight!" said she, smiling at Ernest and everyone who came upon them. "Once I have washed the smell of fish off me!" She was laughing, her face full of tangled hair.

Happy chatter accompanied the sound of carts going over the stony path, taking the barrels to the storage barn on the Tremaine estate.

"In view of recent events, I have got another dog; it's a pup, it needed a home and will need training. I thought it could work alongside Hugo," said Ernest.

Looking up from her deep thoughts, "Yes, a good idea, in view of 'recent events'," she replied.

Riding back to the house, Milady was looking up at the sky. "Please, stay dry for tonight!"

"You might be lucky! There's them there clouds over there, but they might blow over."

"Well, as long as I am dry going in, it doesn't matter so much going home," said she, smiling at Ernest. "Do you ever feel things are going too well, and you wait for something or someone to upset the peace?"

Smiling at her very dirty face, Ernest said, "We keep our guard up; it's when you relax, things can take you unawares!"

They rode peacefully home. In the distance, they could still hear a cart rumbling over the stony path. Three tired people rode into the courtyard.

"Mrs West, is everything all right?"

"Yes Milady, I've taken it upon myself to sew that there lace on that green dress you said you was going to wear." She held it up for inspection; there was a little silence; breath held.

"Yes, it's beautiful," said Milady, putting her right hand over her heart. "Oh goodness, what time is it? About three! Can you fill the bath for me in the conservatory, please?" looking at Tabitha. "And Mrs West, could you do the finishing touch to my lovely dress please? I think it'll take a while to get my hair smelling sweet."

Ernest looked up. "Not forgetting your dirty face!" said he, laughing as he escaped out of range.

"Really, you didn't say anything! How long was my face dirty for…? Ernest!" she shouted after him.

He waved. "Not long!"

There was a deep intake of breath by the women in the room, followed by a burst of laughter, then it was back to the business in hand.

"Well, it saves time dragging it upstairs, and with curtains pulled, it's private."

"I'll have your dress finished and ironed for ee."

"Thank you."

Climbing into the hot water she slipped underneath the bubbles. "Ooh, that's welcome!" She gave herself a good scrub, her hair taking most of the time. She soaked herself for an hour, then getting out of the bath on to the cold stone floor wrapped the towel around her body. She got nearer the fire, now with the smaller towel around her head. She was feeling excited.

"Let's dry your hair by the fire," said Tabitha.

"I hope Sophia is back from her foreign travels with her stories to tell; if she is, I have not been informed though." She was thinking out loud to Tabitha who was busy with Elizabeth's hair, and Matilda was busy with the children in the garden.

Her hair was nearly dry, and with Tabitha's help, her under petticoats were on. Tabitha was putting ribbons and beaded pins in her mistress's hair.

"How is Jonas? Any change in your plans?"

"No, Milady, he wants to be the head groom first, so he has better money."

"Ahh! He has plans! Very sensible."

Milady's hair was high on her head, with curls around neck and face. "You look as pretty as a picture, if I may say so, Milady."

"Thank you, Tabitha, I must admit I do feel good tonight."

"Here is your dress, Milady," said Mrs West.

"The cream lace looks so right on that shade of green." Slipping the freshly ironed dress over her head, she added, "I forgot how much I loved this dress, I haven't worn it since before Charles was born, so three and a half years ago."

"And the moths haven't killed it!" All laughed together. "Covering your dresses seems to work," said Tabitha.

"At what hour are you leaving?"

"Seven o'clock. Ernest is taking me in the buggy, I don't think horseback will do tonight." There was a burst of laughter, from the three women.

A gloved hand held up assisted Milady into the carriage. She picked up her dress sufficiently to lift her foot without tripping. "Thank you Ernest." A cream lace shawl encrusted with stones, from the legacy left by her mother, lay across her slim shoulders. The door was shut, Ernest climbed onto his seat and they were off.

A gentle breeze caused a slight chill in the air. Feeling a shudder, she thought, *is it the cold or anticipation of seeing Charles? The journey seems to take forever.*

And then they were there. Pulled up in the drive way were carriages of all sizes and degrees of wealth. Large oil lamps were lighting the way; the scene was splendid indeed.

"If this is the outside, the indoors must be really spectacular," said she, feeling like a child going to her first party. "I cannot remember it looking so grand," she added, looking up at the large house. As children Sophia and Elizabeth didn't notice as they ran around the house and grounds, playing hide-and-go-seek. I can remember the last time I was home.

Sophia had been away in France this last year. "I do so miss her!" She looked at Ernest.

"I will wait with the other men, Milady, for when you are ready to go home."

"Thank you, Ernest." He helped her out of the carriage.

Though feeling a bit conspicuous walking in unaccompanied, she was holding her head up. "Elizabeth! Elizabeth!" Looking around she saw a gloved hand waving over the heads, finally, pushing her way through the crowd Elizabeth wrapped her arms around her dear friend.

"When did you come back? I hoped you would be back for tonight!"

"I arrived home today, I thought I would surprise you!"

"Well you have! How was Paris?" said she hugging her friend.

"Wonderful! They could not quite get the 'country girl' out of me... There is unrest in Paris though, and it was so smelly, the people are starving... I was glad to come home, I did so miss the sea air and I was so home sick. After a while the balls get wearisome, so here I am!"

Smiling, Elizabeth said, "Yes, I can see that and I am so glad you are here," hugging her dear friend, "so Sophia, what are your ambitions now? Do you have any suitors?"

"A husband! I am not getting any younger," said she, looking around as though a likely candidate were about.

Sophia was a year younger than Elizabeth. Her fiancé died so her father sent her off to Paris to 'find herself'. It would appear to have worked; she was happy and bubbly. Walking into the grand hall Sophia was oblivious to her surroundings, but Elizabeth was in awe, trying not to look too childish.

"Ooh, this is beautiful, Sophia!" She followed Elizabeth's gaze. "The ceiling? Yes I suppose it is. But what wouldn't I give to have a husband and children!" said she, looking forlorn for the first time.

Elizabeth looked at her friend, now clutching her hand. "How selfish of me!" said Sophia, "you lost your husband, how have you been? You look beautiful!"

"I am happy now the children have settled, they do not mention their father, so I do not. They are so young. Anyway, it is about you tonight!" she said, kissing her dear friend's cheek. "I am so glad you are home, now let's look at the young men!" The smile immediately was back on her perfect sculptured little face.

"Ladies!" Feeling a chill up her spine, she recognised that voice.

"Charles!" She turned around. A smile crossed his face. Taking her hand he kissed it, for a little longer than etiquette required.

Feeling flushed Elizabeth said, "May I introduce my dear friend, Miss Sophia Bennett?" Her hand was given and kissed gently.

"Sophia, may I introduce Mr Charles Long?"

"Ladies! May I escort you both into the assembly?"

"You may, sir," each tucking a hand under his elbows. They walked into the glittering assembly towards the reception line.

"Well, well, here they are, beautiful young women, and... Good gracious, sir, you have commandeered both!" Mr Bennett was laughing in a jolly manner. Introductions were made. "Now young ones, go off and enjoy yourselves... Mr Long, a word in a while, if you please."

Charles nodded, looking now concerned. "Yes Mr Bennett."

Violins played a new tune from France; humming along Sophia informed the duo that she had heard it many a time at the many balls she frequented.

Looking at Charles's face Elizabeth suddenly felt ill at ease. "Is everything well? You look perplexed."

"I have some business to which I must attend, so I will be leaving tonight," said he, looking into Elizabeth's face.

"Will you be coming back?"

"Yes I will, and Elizabeth...you must be vigilant!" He caught her hand.

She looked into his face. "You are worrying me now, Charles."

"One dance first, Elizabeth." Looking up into his eyes she was trying to read his mind, but as usual she could not see through that hard exterior. She was feeling puzzled but determined not to become emotional. She knew something was going on, out of her control.

The dance finished. "I thought you couldn't dance!" said she, smiling.

"I found it not too hard to follow."

Sophia came tripping back and whispered into Elizabeth's ear. "So many young men, but I don't know them!" Just then Mr Bennett nodded to Charles, who turned to the ladies. "Elizabeth... Miss Sophia..." He gave a nod and was gone; his back was in view as he pushed his way through the now crowded room.

"Let's get a drink... Punch?"

"Yes please." They made their way to the drinks table. Sophia spoke to the servant while Elizabeth looked around. She caught a glimpse of Charles, looking as if he knew she was looking, he turned around and smiled, then he was gone, lost in a sea of suits and dresses.

Sophia was standing, holding two glasses. "Are you walking out with Mr Long?"

Turning around, Elizabeth said, "No, no...we are just friends! I would like more, but I have been widowed. Less than a year."

"A very handsome friend. We don't get the chance in love often, Elizabeth, so if it feels right then, my dear friend, please tell him. Any gossip will cease, people will forget, your reputation may be bruised but not permanently damaged." Now Sophia looked to be on the verge of tears.

Elizabeth locked her arm with her friend's. "So who have you been looking at?" Elizabeth was determined not to be sullen on such a grand occasion; her dear friend was back, with stories to tell.

"Milady."

"Monsieur Carnot, how are you, sir?" Before he had a chance to answer, "May I present Miss Sophia?"

Taking her hand and kissing very gently, "*Enchanté*, Mademoiselle!" he said.

"So Monsieur, how are you enjoying your visit to Cornwall?"

"Beautiful countryside! My business has been interesting and is now completed, so I will be on my way back shortly."

"Monsieur, would you like to join us in a game?" asked one of the guests. Bowing, he said, "Ladies, if you can forgive me," and he was gone. They watched him go into the games room.

"That's it. It is official, there is a shortage of eligible men."

"Well, has anyone caught your attention?" Elizabeth asked, subtly looking around. "Are there any eligible men here? Your father invited these guests so I am sure there will be lots of single people."

"Yes, but none have caught my eye... Ooh, who's that!" Just then a tall handsome man stood in the doorway. "He appears to be on his own..." He smiled at them both, but then a pretty young blonde slipped her arm into his. "That's who he was waiting for!" She felt dejected.

"Sophia, there is someone for you!" As if by request Albert appeared. "Albert! May I introduce my dear friend Miss Sophia Bennett? And Sophia...this is Captain Albert Edwards."

He kissed her hand. "Would you like to dance, Miss Sophia, if I may call you that?"

"Yes you may, and yes, I would... Oh, Elizabeth!"

"You go and have an amusing time. I need to mingle, anyway." She watched them walk away, in conversation. *I wonder,* she thought to herself.

"Elizabeth. A dance, please?" For a moment, there was no one there but Charles in the room, standing tall and handsome. Holding his hand out, he led her onto the dance floor. There was bowing and curtsying, then each man standing opposite his partner, the dance commenced, twirling in and out, changing partners, back to the original partner. Kissing her hand, "That will have to last until I come back," he said.

"I will miss you, do come back safely. Where are you going; can you say?"

"I suppose I can. To Plymouth, then sailing to France. When I come back we must talk." Something caught his eye. "I fear I must go," said he, leading her back to her friend, "I thought we were going to have tonight, but time is of the essence."

Sophia was in deep conversation with Albert, "But I am sure there are troubles ahead in Paris; the people are hungry." Albert was about to answer when Elizabeth appeared. Charles kissed Elizabeth's hand once more, and saying his farewell to the little party he was gone.

"Where has Charles gone?"

"Called away on business."

"Do you know what that might be?"

"No! You know I did not ask." The light floating music filled the room.

A flute of champagne was put into her hand. Her composure came back. "Well Albert, is there any news about the highwayman?"

"We have been talking about Paris. What is this about a highwayman?" asked Sophia, looking concerned.

Albert, shifting his weight, said, "Well, there have been attacks, Milady being one."

"Call me Elizabeth, please."

"I will then! Several reports of theft, but he has disappeared. No one has seen him. There is a report of an injured man seen in the woods."

"Let's change the subject."

"But Elizabeth, you didn't tell me!"

"It happened weeks ago, I was just curious if he was caught... "She redirected the conversation. "This French trouble, have you heard anything, Albert?"

"No, it will probably come to nothing."

"I see Mr Long has left us," said Mr Bennett, looking a little the worse for wear, joining the little group. "Yes, tricky business this Paris problem," said he, then realising he was perhaps being indiscreet, "um, um..." Sophia was looking fretful. "Oh, I wouldn't be too sure, Albert, it was quite frightening at times."

"Elizabeth!" Mr Bennett, taking her by the hand, steered her into the games room.

Elizabeth looked around. "Not many ladies present."

"So I see. Well, it's a man's game and ladies do not seem to enjoy games, they would rather dance and talk."

"Let's not forget our drinks, and eat your delicious food," said she. Hearing the boulanger, a dance she loved commencing, "I will leave you to your cards, Mr Bennett." She found her friends in a deep discussion about France.

Albert was quite adamant. "Whatever happens, it is in France and miles away from here. No need to worry that pretty head of yours!" Realising what he'd said, he blushed, but Sophia was enjoying the attention.

Elizabeth was smiling to herself on finishing her drink. "I think I must go, I am feeling rather tired, what with the fishing today as well." Swaying to the tune she was tempted to get Albert to dance, but decided against it.

"Sophia kissed Elizabeth's cheek. "I do not know where you get your vitality."

"No, I don't either, but it seems to have deserted me at present. I will see you soon," said she, holding both of Sophia's hands.

"I presume Ernest is here?"

"Yes, he is in the servants' quarters. I shall go and find him. Come tomorrow and see the children and we can really catch up. Good night, Albert."

"Yes I will, about three in the afternoon."

"I will look forward to it."

A little wave and she was gone, her beautiful green dress floating out behind her.

She found Ernest with the other carriage drivers, standing around a fire, having a drink and conversing. She caught his attention; he waved, said something to the others and left to get the carriage.

Elizabeth was starting to shiver. She pulled her shawl up and around her head. Hearing horses' hoofs, she turned around to see Ernest with the carriage. He jumped down from his seat to open the door; the wind caught her shawl but she just held it in time.

Ernest took her hand and helped her into the carriage. "Thank you, Ernest."

The horse's hoofs were clipping along the dry road, then the rain came, it lashed down, making her mood more sombre.

They arrived home; the journey seemed to take for ever. Opening the door they dashed inside...the house was still, then suddenly Hugo came bounding down the stairs, followed by the patter of little paws. "Hello boys!" she said, patting their heads, "have you been good?" looking directly at Copper who was too busy trying to annoy Hugo. "Get down now. Hugo, you have some teaching to do!" She brushed the invisible fur off her dress.

As she went into the study for a nightcap Ernest appeared.

"A little brandy, Milady?"

"Don't mind if I do!" He poured from the crystal decanter and they clinked glasses.

"Did you have a pleasant evening?" Now all four were sitting by the fire.

"Yes, Sophia is back from Paris, she became 'homesick' and the unrest there upset her. Captain Edwards thinks it will come to nothing. And now Mr Long is going there on business, it seems. I never did ask him what his business was," said she, looking at Ernest and taking a sip of brandy. "I have a feeling you know what's going on; and why would an American have business in Paris? Goodness me, I think I indulged to excess in the champagne. I will retire."

Ernest was stroking the dogs' heads. "Ask him when he comes back. Perhaps all will become clear." Draining his glass, he said, "Come on, boys. I'll make a final check of the house Milady."

The dogs got up, both reluctant to leave the fire. The patter of paws followed Ernest out of the room.

She was left with her thoughts. All will become clear, I wonder what he means by that? Ernest put his hat and coat on, shaking his head. *There's going to be trouble,* he thought to himself.

"Come on boys!" He walked out of the door, the dogs obediently following.

Elizabeth was about to get into bed when a noise outside distracted her. Looking out of the window she burst out laughing. Copper was taking a great interest in the peacocks; their plumes up and squawking loudly, they were chasing the dog which ran back to Ernest with its tail between its legs. Hugo had learnt his lesson years ago and stood there barking at Copper. Opening her window she called, "'Night, Ernest."

Looking up at the window, "'Night, Milady." He waved and the three of them disappeared around the house.

The house and especially the peacocks settled down.

Her head touched the pillow and she was asleep.

Chapter Six

The weather had changed; the trees with their branches blowing in all directions, as if they were trying to clear the old wood; the leaves looked rusty, more brown and orange than green. Elizabeth looked up. *I hadn't noticed,* she thought, *I have been so wrapped in my own little world...autumn is here!* She wrapped her shawl tightly around her.

Elizabeth was walking along the beach, the two children running ahead with Hugo, and Copper who had grown and was not much shorter than Hugo, and there, right before their eyes... He had grown despite time passing so slowly, or so it felt to Milady.

It had been three months since the ball when Sophia came home from Paris. She was walking out with Captain Edwards; there would be wedding bells soon and Elizabeth couldn't be more happy for them both. But though there was nothing from Charles, she felt sure he would return.

Hugo was still teaching Copper who was master, with the odd big paw on the pup's head when he got too playful. Just then Copper nipped Hugo, who in turn got the pup on the sand with his paw on his neck, accompanied by a growl. "All right boys, come on!" shouted Ernest as he beckoned the dogs to him, both dogs sprang up and chased after Ernest who then chased after the children, all joining in laughing as they went.

As sad as she felt, Elizabeth couldn't help but smile. Stopping and looking out to sea, "Where are you, Charles?" she murmured. Just then a gust of wind seemed to circle her. "Ooh," she exclaimed, having to hold onto her bonnet and shawl. Her coat was buttoned up and so was secure. That instant she forgot her misery.

"Mama!"

Looking at her darling daughter, "I am coming," she said, hurrying after her.

Later in the kitchen, she remarked, "Christmas Eve is just over two weeks away; how is your dress coming along, Matilda?"

"Nearly done, Milady. I just need to sew the hem up, then it is finished."

Ernest came into the kitchen, passing Matilda. He was closely followed by both dogs who slumped down in front of the fire. "Are you well, my love?" said he, looking lovingly at Matilda.

"Yes, thank you!" She returned that look as she left the room.

"You two, it's so lovely to have love and happiness around us! There's Miss Sophia's wedding as well, on New Year's Eve. So there are two weddings in two weeks." Looking into his face, "Still no news about the highwayman, Ernest?"

"A rumour has spread about goings-on around Plymouth; it could be him, he could be going further afield, or it's not him and he's dead!"

"Well, wherever he is, it doesn't seem to be here. I still carry my pistol... What is it you say, Ernest? It's when you're not ready that things take you by surprise."

"Yes, that's right, always be on guard," said he, looking at Milady.

"Is everything in order, Ernest?"

"Yes, oh yes! Forgive me, Milady, I was miles away." *And you too,* she thought.

The children came bursting in. "Mama, I have got my sums right!"

Picking the little girl up onto her lap and kissing her hair, "You clever girl!" she said.

Matilda walked in after her, followed by Charles. "I did too, Mama!"

All were now looking at Charles; tall, but still only three years old with a mop of black hair. "Really! You are clever." They all were trying not to giggle at him. "Now tea, then bed."

"But I am not tired!" moaned the little girl.

"No, it is just that the evenings get darker earlier, so tea then bed!"

When tea was finished, Milady said, "Right; upstairs with Matilda and I will be up shortly."

Looking at Ernest she said, "I feel a need to travel. I wonder what France is like? I speak the language so that wouldn't be a problem." She didn't know if she even meant or believed what she was saying.

Ernest looked down at his hands. "I don't think in this weather it's the right time to go oversea," said he, looking into her face. Getting up, "Umm," she said, "I'll think about it," as she walked out of the room.

"I feel trouble coming." Ernest got up, shaking his head. "Where are those dogs?" They'd had enough of the fire and had gone exploring. Ernest could hear them somewhere, paws on the wooden floors. They both came bounding around the corner.

"Come on boys, I need to walk and think."

A man with a musket and two dogs went towards the woods. "Let's find some rabbits for tomorrow's dinner."

Walking up the stairs, the more she thought, *Was it a good idea to go to Paris? I am sure father said we had relatives there, but we lost contact for some reason. Perhaps Ernest was right, a bad time of year to go across the Channel; it will be rough, and I haven't been feeling right and...* Sitting on her bed, and with the realization she had been putting something off, *I haven't had a monthly flow for nearly four months,* she thought, placing a protective hand on her stomach. Putting my head in the sand won't make my problem go way; at least I can hide a little in the winter, but come spring it will be hard to explain, and with no Charles... Her thoughts tailed off.

"Are you well, Milady? Beg pardon, but you look pale." Tabitha had come into the room with her, and she had not noticed.

"I am just tired, I don't like winter and the cold." Tabitha hesitated, and then with a smile was gone. Elizabeth could hear her humming a tune as she went downstairs. Tabitha's good mood was infectious.

Reading with the children was a little more exciting than usual. They had grown weary with the same books, much to the relief of their mother. So they were now reading 'Gulliver's Travels', one of Elizabeth's favourites. She remembered her governess reading it with her. Her darling father was still alive then; she still missed him, his booming voice, the way he tried to keep a straight face when telling her off, and the way he treated other people. Making her way into her cold bedroom she looked out to sea and fought back tears. "Be resolute, Elizabeth, you are a Tremaine!" With her chin up she brushed down her dress on hearing Ernest was back in with the dogs. She made her way downstairs, following them into the kitchen. "I have changed my mind. I think you are right, it is not the weather for travelling oversea."

Ernest looked relieved. *That is just as well,* he thought to himself. *I didn't wish to tell her why it wouldn't be safe, not just yet.*

She was stroking Hugo's head and of course Copper needed affection too. Coming over to her he nuzzled her leg to get her attention, making her smile. "That's better, Milady, I haven't seen you smile much these last few months, if I may say so."

Do I tell him or not, she thought. He has cares enough at the moment. "No, I have been feeling sad but with two weddings taking place and of course Christmas, my mood will improve greatly, I am sure of it!"

Ernest changed the subject. "I have seen a handsome tree for the parlour, on the edge of the woods." These woods were Mr Bennett's; he would not mind, but she didn't want to take advantage of him. He had been a great comfort since her father's death, and when she was married he guided her, although she went against his advice, and married a scoundrel. "I know Mr Bennett would not mind, but we had better make sure."

"I will, Milady."

"Do you want children, Ernest?"

"If God willing. I know Matilda does."

There was silence for a few seconds, although it felt longer.

"So when the weather is dry, you'll get the tree? I must visit the village too, for the last of my Christmas shopping." *And a visit to her doctor,* she thought to herself. She was not looking forward to this with his opinions; he would need to keep silent.

Ernest delayed answering. "We could be waiting a long while for dry weather," said he laughing, "I'll get the tree and leave it in the outhouse, next to the kitchen, until it has dried out somewhat."

Elizabeth was feeling brighter and entering the Christmas spirit. "That sounds like a good idea. I'll cut some holly tomorrow with Tabitha. Time has passed so quickly."

Both went into the office. She said smiling, "A drink, Ernest?" Holding the decanter in her hand she added, "Will we have enough 'goods'. To last us over Christmas?"

He was looking into his glass, as though it had the answer!

"Yes, it should last." Now he was relaxing in the chair opposite the desk.

Trying to act in a casual manner and looking at Ernest's face, "Any news concerning Mr Long as yet?" she asked.

"I haven't heard anything but I am not privy to that sort of information, and I have heard no gossip." Drinking up, he said, "'Night, Milady, early start tomorrow!"

"Yes, good night, Ernest."

A little later, taking a candle and making her way up the stairs, she could hear Hugo scratching around. He still slept outside her room. Copper slept downstairs with Ernest, about which she was glad as he didn't settle very quickly and was very playful. "'Night boy," she murmured, bending down to touch his coarse fur and getting a lick in return. She looked in the children's room; both were asleep. Going into her room Elizabeth left the door open a little, she'd done that since Amelia and Charles were born.

She went to the window to look at the night sky. It was dark and dismal, she couldn't see any stars, only dark clouds filled the sky, and even the peacocks were quiet. "Ooh!" She put a hand to her belly. "A life!"

It was letting her know it was there, and it was not going to go away any day soon. Ernest was up early and had gone when the rest of the house woke up. "Mrs West, did you see Ernest this morning?" asked a yawning Elizabeth.

"Yes, Milady, he be gone to see Mr Bennett, then something about a tree."

"Capital! Ah, Tabitha, do you fancy a walk after breakfast to get holly and wood? We could take the children; fresh air will do them good, we'll wrap up warm." She looked out of the window. "It's dry at the moment." Voices were coming down the corridor. "Stop arguing, children!"

"Matilda! Tabitha and I are taking the children out near the woods, to collect holly and wood. Do you feel able to come? The dogs too, of course." *And my pistol,* she thought, *but I won't mention that.*

"Yes, Milady."

"Good! The more hands the merrier, breakfast first!"

They had a hearty breakfast of meat with bread, warm milk for Amelia and Charles, and tea for the adults. Later in the hallway, there was the hustle and bustle of three adults and two children getting dressed in the correct attire for the cold wind: boots, hats and gloves, and of course the winter coats. "But I don't want to wear my coat!" Charles was moaning and wriggling.

"But Charles, it is cold! You'll be glad of it when you're outside."

He relented and stood still. "Oh, all right then."

"That's my little soldier!" Milady ruffled his hair then pulled his hat down over his head.

The collection of holly usually marked with no problems, except this year Amelia cried when she held the holly too tightly, but with a kiss and a hug all was forgotten. "I think we have got enough for Mr Bennett's house as well!" The women each walked with a basket full of holly bearing red berries.

Tabitha looked concerned. "Now young Charles; these," she said, pointing to the berries, "are not to be eaten, they will make you poorly!"

"No, I won't touch." The children ran ahead with sticks in their hands, waving them around, taking the tops off any plant brave enough to have its head above the soil.

"It is not that I do not trust him, but keep it out of his reach. I can see mischief in his face."

"Yes Milady, I can too!" smiled Matilda, who probably knew the children better than anyone.

"The weather is holding so I am going to the village," announced Milady. Everyone was in the kitchen now, with the children warming themselves by the fire.

"May I ride along with you, Milady? I have some things to do and I don't like going alone this time of year," said Tabitha.

"Yes, of course you may, it will be pleasant to have company," said she smiling, but her mind was working overtime. I will have to be careful going to the doctor. The whole house will know about my visit, and will think that I am ill, or worse, will deduce the true reason…

Dan saddled Star and a little good-tempered horse for Tabitha. She did not ride much; in fact Elizabeth could not remember a time when she did.

Both women sat astride the horses going at a slow trot into the village and chatting as they went. After the horses were stabled Elizabeth said, "Right, I have some business to attend to, I shall meet you in The Tavern for lunch in an hour."

"Yes, Milady." Elizabeth wandered away looking around the shops, and over her shoulder to see if Tabitha was nearby, but she was not in sight. "Right, Doctor Mactavish," murmured Elizabeth. The physician had a room for consultation on the first floor of his house, his wife was the receptionist and nurse. *I just hope she keeps her own counsel,* she thought. This is my secret to tell, when I am ready. The house stood out from the row of cottages by a plaque outside stating Doctor Mactavish.

There were the letters MD and some other initials that had no meaning for her. Finally she was sitting in a waiting room, practising in her head what she was going to say, when the doctor's door opened. "Good day, madam!" The voice caused Elizabeth to look up and straight into the face of Sally Brown, her now deceased husband's mistress. Both women glared at each other. Elizabeth's gaze went to the obviously swollen belly. Her head raced for dates.

"It cannot be my husband's, it's been too long."

"Don't go worrying, it isn't your old man's. I have a gentleman, I do! He's married me, he has!" said she, flashing a ring.

Composure regained and smiling through gritted teeth, "Congratulations!" said Elizabeth, "I would hold onto him, there are women around here that would take him off you. Good day to you!" Elizabeth got up and went into the doctor's surgery.

"You handled that very well, Milady."

"Well, to be quite honest, she did me a favour but I would never tell her that." She could feel herself blushing. "I have a sensitive dilemma," said she, looking into the old man's eyes.

"You know anything you tell me is in confidence. I have taken an oath."

"That is fitting because I am going to need your trust. I am expecting."

If he was shocked, he didn't show it, but now it was his turn to work out dates. "I'll save you the trouble of the calculation…it is a bastard as I am unwed. I haven't worked out how to solve the problem yet, I am about four months gone. The father has gone away and I do not know if he is coming back. Looking down at her hands, "But I can deal with this," she concluded.

Bending down and putting his hands on hers, he said, "We will deal with this, Milady, I promised your father I would look after you, and I will."

Later, on leaving the doctor her heart was not feeling quite so heavy.

"Milady!"

"Oh Tabitha, you startled me!"

"Have you finished your errands?"

"No, I have a little more to do."

"Well, I will walk with you and carry your bags. I have finished my items…" said she, and realising she had overstepped the mark, "forgive me, Milady, if that is acceptable to you?"

Elizabeth was laughing. "Yes, it will be agreeable to have company. You can help me chose a present for Matilda.'

"That's a hard one."

After hesitating over hats, gloves and jewellery, she finally settled on material. "I think Matilda will like this material; there is enough for two dresses if she so desired."

"She will love the colour, and she said the other week her wardrobe was looking pitiful."

Payment was made. Money was not such a worry since the pilchards were sold to Italy. There were still a good twelve weeks to go before spring, though if the weather allowed, the farmers could start work in the fields. In the meantime, she had to be careful, but if all else failed they still had the pilchards, enough to last them all.

"And Ernest? What to get him?"

"I know, a pipe! A man can never have too many!" Laughing, she said she had already bought him a cap but it didn't seem enough.

Outside The Tavern she exclaimed, "Oh Milady, you sure?" hearing men's rowdy laughter.

"Yes, come on Tabitha, we'll find a cosy little corner." She pushed the door open to a smoky atmosphere and the voices died down. "'Morning," she said, smiling sweetly as they made their way in.

"Why have they gone quiet?"

Leaning forward, "It happens all the time," keeping a straight face but could contain no more. Milady smiled and lent forward to whisper, "I don't know; perhaps they were talking about a delicate matter and they didn't expect to see two ladies of consequence walk in."

Now it was Tabitha's turn to laugh. She was bursting to tell Elizabeth something. "Jonas has got the head groundsman's position...now we can get married!"

Looking into her sweet young little face, Elizabeth reached out and holding one of her hands, "I am so happy for you!" said she, choking back a tear.

"Oh Milady, it's all right!"

"I am aflutter with happy news." Changing the subject quickly, "Have you named the day yet?"

"Yes, spring time we are thinking." The Tavern livened up again with a song with words about smugglers and highwaymen; it made Milady's hair stand on end.

They had some sort of stew to eat and ale to wash it down, then they were on their way. "Beg pardon, how about you, Milady?" asked Tabitha, looking into her face.

"No, I have no love interest." *Not lying,* she thought, *I don't know where he is or if he is even alive.*

The horses were collected. The journey home started well and then it began to rain, and it really did rain. "Typical! We will get drenched." So they moved a little quicker, on the verge of a gallop, but they both knew it was a slippery path when wet. "At least it is not snowing!" shouted Milady, trying not to get her hair too wet, as she pulled her hood further over her bonnet.

The journey seemed to take forever, but finally the gates were in sight, and Ernest and Dan appeared from the barn. "We wondered when you'd be home," said Ernest as he helped Milady down and taking her water-tight packages from her.

"Thank you for your company, Tabitha."

83

"You're welcome, Milady." A little curtsy and she was gone inside, followed quickly by Milady and Ernest.

"Master Charles has been sick, we think he ate some of them there berries."

"How bad?"

"Well, he's been so sick I don't think he's got anything left inside his little body to come out!"

"Oh my!" Elizabeth rushed to the stairs, taking her coat off as she went and throwing it on a nearby chair. She ran upstairs two at a time, lifting her skirt up so as not to fall, with Ernest hot on her heels. They went into the nursery and she was met by Dr Mactavish.

"It is all right my dear! In my opinion, he has brought it all up, and what he hasn't will pass though him fairly quickly," said he, now looking at the little boy, as pale as his sheets, with his black hair as a contrast.

A tear rolled down her face. Dr Mactavish put an arm around her shoulders. "Now I see no reason why he won't be running around as usual in a couple of days. Children tend to be restored quickly."

"I know…he just looks so ill!"

"Mama! Sorry mama." Going to his side she touched his cold, clammy forehead. "You silly boy, you've worried us all." Bending down and kissing his face, "You sleep!" she murmured, and as if on command he closed his eyes and was asleep.

"I am sorry, Milady! I left them on the table, I didn't think he would touch them." Matilda looked haggard, and whatever anger Milady had felt just melted. She hugged the woman. "We must be vigilant; he is a mischievous child. I think this is the first of many incidents to come. Keep out of reach any harmful plants, get rid of the berries although I don't think he will do this one again," all looking down on his white face.

"No, I don't think he will." Matilda was shaking her head.

"We couldn't find you in the village, so I called the doctor and hastened back."

"Thank you Ernest!"

Feeling guilty she added, "We were having a meal in The Tavern after making our purchases."

"I must have been one step ahead of you, because I went in there."

"Well, he has been seen by the doctor now, and you did the right thing as always, Ernest! I don't know where I'd be without you." She gave him a hug; he looked embarrassed, then nodding, put his cap on and was gone.

"I'll sleep in here tonight, Milady, just to be near if Master Charles wants anything."

"Thank you, yes; a wise suggestion."

Making her way downstairs she remembered she was still wet from the rain, so turning around went back upstairs to change her clothes. Later, sitting in the office by the fire with both dogs laid out like furry rugs, she was taking a sip of wine, and almost nodding off to sleep when a heavy knock came at the old oak door. She jumped up to answer it herself. Ernest was hot on her heels.

"I'll see to it, Milady!"

"I am there now, Ernest."

"Mr Bennett, how nice to see you! Sophia!"

"We heard Master Charles was sick, so here we are with an armful of fruit and a bottle of something."

"Come in." Elizabeth put her arm in her friend's while Ernest and Mr Bennett were left talking in the hallway. She took Sophia's coat.

"So how is he?"

"We think he's eaten some berries from the holly that we had collected earlier in the day. It made him rather sick, but Dr Mactavish has seen him and is happy with his progress. He thinks the poison will work its way out... Both ends... If anything had happened to him, I would not have forgiven myself."

Sophia was now sitting beside Elizabeth, putting her arm around her shoulder.

"There, there. Boys will be boys. So they say!"

"I know, and he is going to be well again. Thank goodness he didn't eat any more. Would you care for some wine, Sophia?"

"Yes please."

"How are your wedding arrangements?"

With two glasses in hand Elizabeth gave one to Sophia who, taking a sip, said, "Well! All is arranged; we are having a pre-wedding dinner the Saturday before. You will come, won't you?"

"I would love to, unless Charles falls out of a tree, or any of those 'boy things'."

"Didn't you used to climb trees with Ernest as a child?"

"Yes, and you would be standing at the bottom of the tree, shouting for me to come down and be 'a lady'!" She was now laughing, the recent worries forgotten for a while. "Um, um..." Mr Bennett came into the study. Ernest had disappeared.

"Would you like a drink?"

"Yes, please. Do you have any of that fine brandy you served a while ago?"

"Yes I do," said she, pouring him a drink. *I am sure he knows where it came from,* she thought.

"Have you heard from Charles as yet?" asked Sophia.

"No," said she, looking into the fire, "he is probably busy."

Whispering, Sophia said, "Father has not said anything, either."

"We shall see." She was itching to tell her about her news, but Sophia would get excitable and she might betray a confidence; Elizabeth was not ready to face any opprobrium as yet.

"Have you seen your beautiful tree yet?"

"No, I must confess I haven't, what with purchases for Christmas in the village, then Charles's little escapade, but I will in the morning."

"If I say so myself, it's a beauty."

After an evening of entertainment with her two dear friends she found herself checking the downstairs windows. Ernest hearing movement came down to investigate.

"Milady?"

"Ernest, I have checked the study. I was just going to the kitchen and outhouse."

"I'll do that." Both dogs were eager to go out for their last constitutional before bed; Copper didn't bother the peacocks any more, not after they chased and caught him.

"Do you think the tree will be dry for decorating tomorrow?"

"You mean today?"

"Is it that time already? No wonder I am feeling tired."

"Yes, the tree will be ready for the morning. Good night, Milady!" He smiled and went with the dogs towards the kitchen. She could hear him talking to them, making her smile.

She went to check on the children, all were asleep even Matilda, who had a comfortable chair beside Charles, with her feet up on his bed.

Walking gingerly to her bedroom so as to avoid the creaky floor boards she pulled the curtains back to look out to sea. All seemed quiet, there was a crispiness in the air, snow was coming.

Ernest was in the grounds; he'd checked on Dan and all was well, but he still had this uneasy feeling that something was amiss. "Be extra vigilant, boys; there's a storm abrewing."

Chapter Seven

It was the morning of the pre-wedding dinner.

"Which dress will you be wearing, Milady?" *Whichever one fits my growing body,* she thought.

"The blue dress, I have not worn it for a while."

"Weren't you expecting Master Charles when you wore this?"

"Was I? Get out the pale blue one as well; I will try both to see which one is most comfortable."

The Christmas tree had been decorated the day after Charles swallowed the holly berries. He admitted it the same day as he wanted to help dress the tree, and Milady said he could if he told the truth, which he did.

"I saw the red berries on the table and wanted a taste, only one or three. They didn't taste nice, I swallowed them, I didn't mean to!" Now he was well and truly back to normal, and as cheeky as ever.

Elizabeth went down into the kitchen and found Ernest sitting at the table.

"I am going to the cottages, Ernest. Have you any message for Matt?"

"No, Milady, I'll come with ee and see him myself."

Horses were saddled and away they went. Ernest, looking straight ahead, said, "Milady, there's a rumour again about someone loitering around the woods. I don't think it's safe for women to be out alone. Mr Bennett said the other night that a man had been chased off but he could come back, and we still do not know what happed to the highwayman." Now he was looking at her worried face.

"Ernest, there's something I must tell you..." said she, trying to think of the easiest words.

"Morning!" Captain Edwards appeared from behind them."

"Good morning to you too," said Ernest, "where are you off to?" looking behind him to see a dozen bright red uniforms.

"Mr Bennett has asked us to check the woods and environs. There is evidence someone has been living rough, and a deer was slaughtered and half eaten."

"Been there a while, then."

"Yes, it looks like it. I shall have the honour of seeing you tonight, Milady... Ernest." He touched his hat and was gone.

"Such a splendid sight, but you can see them a mile off! Anyone living rough will be long gone," said Milady.

"What were you going to tell me?" asked Ernest, looking a little uncomfortable, as though he wasn't ready for what she was going to say. Milady looked into his worried face.

"It can wait, Ernest."

They approached the row of cottages; children were playing outside. Matt came out to see why the dogs were barking. "Morning, Milady!" said he. Ernest helped her down.

"I need a word, Matt."

"And I'll find Lottie," said Milady.

She knocked on the little cottage door. "Come in, I heard you arrive, Milady."

"Don't get up."

The young woman had an ample breast out. "He's a hungry one, he is!" said she, feeling a little embarrassed at having her breast exposed. "There's hot water on the coals if you would like tea."

"I would, please! Would you like some too?"

"Yes, if you please."

Tea was made. Milady didn't ask how they could afford such an expense as tea, but after all she had brandy and she suspected the tea also came from an untaxed source.

Now sitting up and more comfortable the baby had finished feeding for the moment. "He wants feeding all the time," said Lottie.

"I like his name."

"Well, if it's good enough for King George, then it's good enough for my little George." She put the contented baby over her shoulder, and he obliged with a loud belch. "Good boy!"

The cottage was lovely and warm; the fire was blazing. "You will need that fire, I think snow is coming," remarked Milady.

"I like snow, it's pretty; when I am dressed for it!" Lottie took a sip of tea. "How's Master Charles now? I heard he was poorly."

"Yes, he ate holly berries, I don't think he will be doing that again," both women laughed, now he was out of danger Milady saw the funny side of it. Looking lovingly at baby George she said, "Can I hold him?"

"Yes, be careful Milady he isn't sick on you."

"It doesn't matter. Hello Master George! He's nearly putting his whole little hand in his mouth! I see what you mean, he's hungry still."

But not screaming yet! Milady put him up to her neck and snuggled into him.

"Are you broody? Beg pardon, Milady!"

Looking at Lottie, she replied, "A little; mine are growing so fast."

Then George realised he was hungry and gave out a good hearty cry. Milady handed him back. "He needs his mama. I'll leave you to some peace and quiet, I'll see you nearer Christmas." Closing the door quickly behind her the cold air struck and she pulled her shawl around her head. She walked towards Ernest, and he smiled. "Are you finished visiting for today?"

"Yes, I am done, I have been in a nice warm cottage; now I am feeling the cold."

"Let's get home, Milady," said he, hoisting her up on the horse.

"Thank you, Ernest." The horses slowly made their way over the now slippery path. "Are you all right Ernest? You are very quiet."

"I haven't been to a dinner at Mr Bennett's before. We speak an' all, but this is different."

It never occurred to her that he might be ill at ease. "Are you worried about the meal?"

"No Milady, I know about etiquette. It's just the matter of making polite conversation…"

He had been such a strong influence in her life; she had never seen a weakness before. "Stay with me and if anyone disrespects you… I'll shoot them! I haven't shot anyone for a while."

The worry on Ernest's face was gone as he laughed. "Will you really shoot them?"

"Yes, no one hurts my friends!"

"Best I make sure your pistol is clean then!" Both burst into laughter. Looking at Ernest in profile she felt a surge of sisterly love for him.

Arriving back at the house all was quiet, except for a clinking noise in the barn where it sounded like Dan was hard at work.

Ernest took the two horses as Milady went indoors. She could hear voices coming from the conservatory; it was Matilda teaching the children. She quietly tiptoed past so as not to disturb them.

"Tabitha, will you get a bath ready please, in my room."

"I will do it," said Ernest.

"You came in quickly!"

"Yes, Dan has all in hand, he is staying in here tonight with the dogs until we get back."

"We won't be late, it is a dinner, not an assembly meeting."

Lying back with her body stretched out as much as the bath would allow, she thought not of the past but the present; the future would take care of itself. Her unborn child agreed with her as gentle flutters went across her belly. She smiled as she tenderly touched her flesh, tracing the baby's movements.

Getting out she dried herself, put her cream chemise on and was sitting to put on her stockings and shoes. A light knock came at the door. "Milady, it's Tabitha."

"Come in, just in time for my stays, please," said she, putting her arms up and Tabitha began tightening the corset.

She was tying the ribbons at Milady's back. "Ooh, not too tight! I am sitting down all evening eating, I will need room to breathe as well!" Her breasts were modestly showing.

She was feeling flushed and uncomfortable, this was going to be a long evening. She put the pale blue dress on and actually it was quite comfortable, much to her surprise. Later, her hair done, there was a present in her hands, and she was looking at the neat parcel. *What do you give the girl that has everything? I hope they will like crystal glasses!*

Ernest appeared from his part of the house with both dogs at his heels. "You look very handsome, Ernest." He had dark beige matching britches and jacket, a waistcoat of a darker colour, his white shirt with frills completed with a cravat and of course his tricorne hat.

"Thank you, Milady. I haven't worn these old clothes for… I can't remember how long."

Matilda came in behind him. "The next time will be the two weddings, and if the moths didn't get 'em."

"I guess you covered earnests suits as well?"

"Yes I cover all if not used much." Matilde gave Ernest a kiss on the cheek and they went out. Dan had brought the horse and buggy around. He got down to hand the reins to Ernest, who was helping Milady into the carriage. A final word to Dan and they were off. Looking back at her house Milady saw Dan go inside and she gave a little sigh of relief.

"It will be fun, Albert is a 'working-class gentleman' and some of his friends will be there. I do not know who Sophia has invited, but if required I have my pistol!" said she, looking at Ernest. He laughed, keeping his eyes on the road.

"Thank ee, Milady!"

She touched his arm. The journey was uneventful, and they arrived at the grand house, the large oil lamps burning steadily despite the cold wind gaining strength.

Ernest was not used to handing the reins to another, but he did so, giving Milady his arm and they walked in to be greeted by the butler.

"Good evening sir, madam," said he, bowing slightly and taking their coats.

"Milady, Ernest, grand this is going to be, a lovely evening, an intimate little gathering of family and friends!" exclaimed Mr Bennett.

Kissing her hand he looked so happy; in fact, she mused, *I don't think I have ever seen him quite so happy.*

"Elizabeth, Ernest! Come in!"

"Thank you." They took a glass of wine from the tray offered to them.

"May I take Ernest away from you please, Milady?" Albert bowed.

"Please call me Elizabeth, we are nearly a family now."

The happiness in the room was contagious; laughter and happy voices, of course helped along with the flow of wine.

Later, Elizabeth was sitting opposite Ernest and in between two red-coated gentlemen who were extremely charming.

They were on their third or fourth course. "May I say, Mr Bennett, a grand dinner," said someone. *I am so glad my stays are not too tight,* thought Elizabeth to herself.

"Nothing is too good for my darling Sophia," said Mr Bennett, putting a loving hand over Sophia's. She was looking adoringly at Albert; she turned back to smile sweetly at her father.

"Mr Bennett, this French problem, will it affect trade?" shouted a man down at the end of the table, asking a little louder than he intended. The table went quiet, and he blushed. "Beg pardon, I did not mean to disturb everyone else!"

Mr Bennett looked taken aback. "I have a man taking care of my business, but I think we should discuss this matter another time!" *I wonder if this man is Charles,* thought Elizabeth.

"Yes, of course." The man appeared to slide down out of sight, they didn't hear another word from him for the rest of the evening; in fact he disappeared into a room with Mr Bennett when some guests were stretching their legs.

Elizabeth glanced at Ernest. He looked at ease. No need to use my pistol then, she murmured, smiling to herself.

The evening was a great success. The pleasantries concluded they were on their way home.

Nearing home Ernest asked, "Do you have your pistol?"

"Yes," said she, hiccupping, "I am going to suffer tomorrow!" She was holding her head. "Why do you want my pistol?"

"Better to be safe, Milady."

She rummaged through her bag for it, he took it from her and put it into his jacket pocket. She felt frightened now he was so serious. "Is there something I should know?" she exclaimed, looking around into the darkness.

"No! I'm just being careful!"

"Then why are we suddenly going faster?"

She couldn't understand his calmness. Looking behind them, a movement caught her eye. "Ernest!"

"I know!" Keep your head down!" he shouted, whipping up the horses with the reins, they did as bidden and sped up! The rider now didn't care about being seen; he was hot on their heels.

"Give me the pistol, Ernest! You concentrate on the road and I'll... We have one shot." She now felt absolutely sober. Taking the pistol from Ernest she exclaimed, "I'll wait till he's closer," aiming the pistol at the rider. The clouds partially cleared the moon, he evidently saw the pistol and in a moment his horse slowed he went into the trees. "He's gone to the right into the trees."

The horses continued to race until they reached the house. They pulled up outside as Dan came out. "Are you all right?" he cried, looking at the panting horses and the pale face of Milady who promptly vomited as she got out of the coach

Wiping her mouth, "Pardon me," she panted, "a rather bumpy ride after too much food." Now, though feeling better because her stomach was empty, she wasn't sure about her head after she moved and felt dizzy; she held it as she walked into the house.

"We were chased by a rider on a black horse." Ernest told Dan.

"I wonder if it's the same man. We had a visitor on a black horse and wearing a black coat. He asked to speak to Milady; I think he was French."

Ernest stopped what he was doing. "Did he say anything else?"

"No, then he was gone."

Putting a firm hand on Dan's shoulder Ernest said, "We need to be vigilant... I don't think he means us well."

Dan nodded. "You're right, I'll get the peacocks out and keep an eye open tonight with Lucy." That was his musket; his pride and joy. The excitement was outside, the house was quiet; all were asleep until Matilda came down the stairs. "How was the evening, Milady?"

"Lovely!"

"You look pale."

"I feel pale. I overindulged, and we were chased home over bumpy ground. I've been sick; I need water to clear up the mess at the front."

Matilda listened intently. "I'll do it now while it's safe; Ernest is out at the front."

"I'll come with you!"

"No, you go to bed, Milady!" turning her mistress around and respectfully steering her towards the stairs.

"Thank you; for once I won't argue with you; good night."

Her head touched the pillow and she was asleep, dreaming of faces, laughter, horses and blood. She woke with a start; it was still dark, the house was quiet. She could hear birds, somewhere close. She got up shivering and put a shawl over her shoulders. Looking out of the window she could see dew was settling on the lawn; she couldn't see the peacocks. *Even they sleep,* she thought, smiling to herself.

Hugo was in his usual place, and he lifted his head. "You can stay there, it's early yet." Tiptoeing down the creaky stairs, Elizabeth made her way to the kitchen. Hugo had changed his mind; he was up and racing down the stairs. "You'll wake the whole house!" she murmured, stroking his warm head.

The fire was started and water put on to heat up. Ernest came in. "A little early for you, Milady?" he muttered, rubbing his eyes.

"Yes, I couldn't get back to sleep; have you slept at all?"

"A little, Copper kept growling so I'd get up to have a look, I think it was just wild animals."

"I didn't hear Hugo move and he never does anything quietly!" As though the dog knew she was talking about him, he rested his head on her lap.

"Two days until Christmas Eve and the wedding, I have a lot to do, presents to drop off at the cottages."

A loud knock came at the heavy front door. Everyone in the kitchen jumped, and both dogs started barking. Ernest rushed to the door, Milady's pistol in hand, which he had grabbed on the way from her bag.

"Who is it?" shouted Ernest.

"A message from Captain Edwards!" said the voice on the other side of the door. Ernest gave a deep sigh and opened the door, to see a red-uniformed man standing there with a few others, still on their horses.

"Sir, a note from Captain Edwards."

"Thank you. Is he expecting a reply now?"

"He didn't say."

Ernest opened it, keeping the young man on the doorstop. Reading quickly, he said, "No need for a reply, thank you. Tell him I will deal with it." He shut the door, trying to do so quietly, but with the dogs barking it was probably too late.

"What was it?"

"Just a warning about a stranger in the neighbourhood, asking about you, Milady."

"Ooh! I wonder who that is. And why?" She was feeling a little anxious, but didn't say so.

They heard the sounds of the two children waking up and coming down the stairs.

"Mama!"

"Hello, my darlings!" said she, picking Charles up and swinging him around, kissing his cheek. His little arms wrapped tightly around her neck, he was imprinting sloppy wet kisses over her cheeks. "Come on, let's have some breakfast," she continued, carrying the little boy into the kitchen and putting him into his chair.

Soon, dressed and ready to take her presents around, "Ernest, are you ready?" she enquired.

"Yes; have you got your pistol, Milady?"

"As always," said she, taking it out of her bag, "Here!"

The usual instructions were issued: the house to remain locked up, Dan to keep vigilant and both dogs allowed to roam the house.

Arriving at the cottages, there was a sigh of relief from Milady. *But,* she thought, *there's the journey back yet.*

She visited Lottie and Matt, and the rest of the families, giving them presents of sweets and fruit, and toys for the children, a tradition her father started as lord of the manor.

The journey back was not so pleasant. The wind came up and whirled around, the noises making Milady feel uneasy.

Ernest looked at her. "Are you all right, Milady?"

"Yes, but let's get back."

The journey seemed to take for ever, but finally they were entering the driveway, with the house in sight.

"Thank goodness for that! I have been feeling quite nervous; do you think he is something to do with the highwayman?"

Looking at her worried face, "No I don't, Milady... We need to talk," he said.

"Yes, we do...we'll meet in the office in a while, when all is settled."

"Yes, Milady."

After their lunch, which Milady found hard to swallow, she pondered the reason why. Was it what Ernest was going to say, or was it what she had to tell him? She would need every adult in the house to help her when her illegitimate baby was born. He was her servant but her best friend, too. She didn't want him to look on her with disgust. Or was it just nature's way of telling her she was with child?

"Ernest," she said, now that both were in the office, "what is it I need to know?"

"My father gave me this letter just before he died. Your father, Lord Tremaine, gave it to him for safe keeping until you were old enough, or the need arose; and with this stranger around, the time has come." Ernest stepped forward and handed her a cream-coloured envelope with a seal on the back.

She was turning it over, as though by so doing, she could see through the envelope. "Oh Ernest, I am almost afraid to open it, do you know what is inside?" she exclaimed, looking into his face, trying to read his thoughts.

"Some of it. I will leave you to read the letter, Milady," said he, "call me when you want to talk." And he was gone.

Sitting down behind the desk she gently opened the flap with her finger, and unfolding the paper she recognised her father's handwriting immediately. Elizabeth touched the writing, holding back a tear.

"My Darling Daughter Elizabeth,

I will be long gone when you read this letter. I have entrusted the contents with my faithful gamekeeper and friend Cooper, and in time his son Ernest.

I know them to be good, honest and faithful friends.

What I am about to tell you will be a shock. You will need the support of your protectors and your close friends. I have taken Mr Bennett into my confidence, he too, has been your protector, of which I am sure, now matters are assuming their place.

The greatest shock will be what I am going to tell you now, my darling Elizabeth.

Your birth mother was not the woman whom you called Mama but the daughter of Louis XV.

That is, Princess Maria Adelaide of the house of Bourbon. I do not know what her title might be when you read this.

Elizabeth put the letter down on her lap and read it again and again.

I entrusted this letter to a friend; that if your safety was in question, or that you might have heard gossip and were of age, you were to read this letter.

The woman you called Mama loved you like her own, she was a good woman.

France was involved in a conflict with America, and it was not a good time for an illegitimate royal baby to be presented at Court, so as your Father I brought you home. There was always a chance that someone for whatever reason might search for you, hence you needed protectors.

I hope this letter finds you safe and well, my daughter.

You always had my heart, your Father."

Putting the letter on the table she stared at it, as though it was going to burst into flames.

"Ernest!"

He appeared at the door. "I didn't go far, Milady," he said.

She pointed to the letter. "Please read it!" He picked the letter up and read quickly, as most of it he knew already.

"My father said it was all to protect you, but he never said why. I knew it was something to do with France, but not this."

Ernest continued, "So I wonder why the man in black was asking about you? And he was French."

"Why did you decide to give me the letter now?"

"The note from Mr Bennett advised me to do so. I am thinking he knows the full story."

"Does Charles Long work for him?"

"Yes."

"Do you know why he is in France?"

Looking at her, he thought how well she was taking all this. "Well, I thought he only took care of Mr Bennett's business affairs in France, but now I wonder."

"What were you going to tell me?" said he, changing the subject.

She said laughing, "Like mother, like daughter, I am with child!" and waited for a reaction.

"Yes, we know. If I may say, Milady, Matilda worked it out, we were waiting for you to tell us."

Now Elizabeth looked surprised. "Nothing passes you all, does it?" said she, smiling, "I suppose you know who the father is, too?"

"Yes, Mr Charles Long."

"Ernest, Ernest!" She was thinking out loud. "So Louis XVI is my cousin! There is trouble brewing in France; it is just as well no one knows my heritage. The royal family are not popular, and according to Sophia some of the people are starving."

"I think you should keep your secret safe, the fewer people who know, the safer you'll be."

"Yes, I think you're right. I wonder if my mother is still alive, and if she ever thinks of me?"

"A drink, Ernest, I think we need one," said she, half-laughing.

"Yes, I think we do." He poured one out for them both. "To the future, Milady!" Ernest said, not quite sure what was in store for them both.

Chapter Eight

There was hustle and bustle in the Tremaine house; it was Christmas Eve and the day of Albert and Sophia's wedding.

Finally the children were ready. Amelia was looking beautiful in her bridesmaid's dress, but stood in the corner, afraid to move in case she got it soiled in some way. Charles was sulking, he wanted to carry flowers behind Sophia too, but he was too disruptive; Elizabeth feared he would jump on Sophia's train. She was feeling melancholy, looking at Ernest and Matilda in their Sunday best; they were standing in the hallway ready; they made a lovely couple. Charles already was getting playful, "Stop it, Charles!" cried a little girl, very close to tears. All now ready the little party got in the carriage. The church had been dressed in red and cream roses with greenery and holly, and looking a very traditional Christmas but doubling for a Christmas wedding. The little party arrived at the small village church. They found their seats, and Milady left Amelia with the other bridesmaids at the church entrance.

The organ music playing abruptly stopped and a bridal march commenced. Everyone stood up, some taking a peek over their shoulders to get a glimpse of the beautiful bride. She did not disappoint, a very proud Mr Bennett had Sophia on his arm, who was looking very much the blushing bride. Her dress was of cream lace stretched over silk, the bodice ending just over her breasts, but the lace went up to her neck and down her arms, and tight into her small waist. Her veil was lacy, held on her hair by a pearl tiara which had been her mother's. The train was long, which caused the little bridesmaids to giggle as they were having difficulty not to stand on it. The five little girls looking like angels were dressed in the same cream silk, with red sashes around their waists and carrying small baskets of red and cream roses.

They were married. After the kiss they came back down the aisle, man and wife. The contrast of the bride's dress with the groom's red uniform was striking.

Elizabeth caught Sophia's hand. "You look lovely!"

"Thank you, I am so happy!" said she, kissing Elizabeth's cheek. The couple walked out of the church towards the carriage under an arch of drawn swords; it made a grand sight.

Albert helped his wife into the carriage. "Mrs Edwards!" said he, kissing her hand, to the delight of the' well-wishers that had gathered outside the church. Both were waving whilst trying to avoid a mouthful of rice.

"I am glad they've run out of rice, it has got everywhere!" giggled Sophia as she shook the rice off her veil.

"See you all at home!" shouted Sophia. "Oh, the bouquet!" She stood up, and, "Ready, ladies!" she called; she closed her eyes and tossed it over her shoulder to the waiting ladies, each hoping it would bring them luck in the marital way.

"Ooh, it's my turn next!" squealed a friend of Sophia's. Sophia scanned the crowd looking for Elizabeth. *I wonder where she is,* she thought. The moment passed and the carriage moved off down the stony path to a fine tea at the manor house.

Elizabeth came out of the church with the vicar, talking avidly. He took her hand, said something, kissed her hand, and was gone. *Where have they gone?* she wondered. Then catching up with the others, she asked, "Did I miss the bouquet throwing?"

"Yes!" smiled the happy recipient, flaunting the flowers to anyone who happened to be in the vicinity.

The snow started falling. "This is going to lie, at least we don't have far to go," said Ernest as he helped all into the carriage. "Blankets up around you!" Milady and Matilda covered the two children. "It is an afternoon tea affair so we won't be out late." So Elizabeth was hoping. "Mr Bennett is well known for his parties that go on into the night, but we have the children, he will not expect us to stay late."

On arriving at the manor, the large oil lamps were lit even in daytime when the nights drew in early; now they were giving off heat and a hissing noise which could be heard as the snow got heavier and tried to settle on the flames. "I'll lay they don't stay lit for long," said Ernest, looking up at the continuous flurries.

They were ushered into the ballroom where the grand table was laid out. "I am hungry, Mama!"

"You can have something in just a minute!" Finding herself in front of the host, she exclaimed, "Mr Bennett! What a grand setting!"

"Well, my dear, it is not every day we have a wedding," said he, leaning in as if to whisper, "and one I am happy with! Captain Edwards is a likeable young man, and I am told will do well in the military service, and most of all, my darling girl loves him and he, her!"

He looked like the cat that got the cream, his thumb in his waistcoat holding his watch chain, checking the time.

"Excuse me, it is time we ate. Ladies and gentlemen, please be seated." The butler had his staff in an organised procession, with trays of delicious smelling food.

The glorious food was eaten. "No hurrying back tonight," she said quietly to Ernest who was sitting back in the chair and feeling full. Amelia and Charles had eaten well; Charles was getting tetchy. "I think he is tired," said she, looking at Ernest.

A servant bent over her shoulder. "Madam, a note for you."

Startled, "Thank you," she murmured. Reading the note she looked around. "Ernest, I won't be a minute," said she, smiling, getting up and making her way to the large doors the servant opened for her. She went through and was looking around.

"Milady," said a man's voice. Turning around she espied a tall man dressed in black, with a white frilly shirt, and roguishly handsome.

"Yes? What is the meaning of this note?" said she, holding up the piece of paper, "and how did you get in here?" *Were you the rider,* she wondered, as he looked familiar... "Have we met?" she asked, deciding to be subtle.

"Milady, so many questions. My master is Mr Bennett. I had a note for you but I kept missing you. Then I chased after you; I saw your pistol and realised it was folly, so I waited till now. I have a letter from Mr Charles Long. He charged me with placing it in your hands, and yours only."

A surge of excitement went through her, but she was trying not to show it. He stepped forward; her hair stood up on her neck, there was no one around if he attacked her, and her pistol was in her bag. He discerned her anxiety. "I am not your enemy," said he, and bowing, he placed the letter on a nearby table and walked away. Turning, he saw her watching him as she picked the letter up.

"Milady!" The voice made her jump.

"Oh, Ernest!"

"Are you all right?"

"Yes, I have solved the mystery of the rider. He wanted to give me this." She was holding up the letter.

"Why didn't he just leave it at the house?"

"He claims it's from Charles Long and he had to give it to me personally." Looking at the writing on the front she felt a little fearful of what it would say. No time like the present. Undoing the seal she glanced over the page; she read quickly, her eyes filling with tears.

"Is all well, Milady?" He resisted the urge to snatch the letter off her.

"Yes, oh yes, as long as he comes back alive! He is in France, guarding someone whose life is in danger, but he says it is not for long and he will be back." She was holding the letter to her chest. Then music sounded out from the ballroom. "It is time to take the children home, Ernest."

Goodbyes said, Albert and Sophia were travelling to Europe in a few days, but at Sophia's request they would be avoiding Paris.

The snow was lying thickly now. "I think we have left in time, Ernest."

"Yes, you could be right." He had things on his mind and was not very talkative on the way home. The journey was slow but uneventful; the children were enlivened on seeing the snow. "Mama, when can I open a present?"

"Too early yet; you must get some sleep first."

"Will I get my soldier toy? I've been good."

Their heads touched the pillows and they were gone, both gone into their own little worlds. "Goodnight, you two."

"Happy Christmas! See you in the morning," she exclaimed, hugging first Matilda, then Ernest. "You're my best friend, Ernest!" she declared, kissing his cheek.

She was feeling emotional, sitting alone by the fire with a glass of brandy in her hand. "To you, Mother, wherever you are, and to you, Charles!"

Hugo came in, stretching. "Hello boy, yes I am coming up now."

Christmas morning! Was it the smell of food caressing her nostrils or the children bouncing on her bed that woke her? Even Hugo joined in and they were all running around excited.

"Okay, I am awake."

"Can I see Mama?"

"We don't know, Ernest won't let us downstairs. He said when you woke up; you're awake, now come on, Mummy."

Pulling her covers back laughing, "Okay, okay," throwing her woollen gown over her shoulders. The children raced downstairs. "Careful," shouted their mother with no avail. Charles tripped on the bottom step, slid across the shiny wooden floor and came to a halt at Ernest's feet. He jumped up rubbing his knees. *They are too excited,* their mother thought, putting her hand to her mouth.

Ernest stood guard on the conservatory door. "Ooh please," looking at Milady, "let's see if there's any pressies," Ernest peeped in, "I can't see anything."

Both stood in disbelief. "There's presents," Ernest smiling and opening the door wide, both ran in to the little piles of parcels they found there; even Hugo and copper had little presents. Paper ripped open, lots of oos and ahhs, it wasn't a lot but it was what they liked... a family tradition of giving loved ones presents at Christmas and was continued by Milady.

Ernest put his cap on, Matilda liked her material, Mrs West put her new apron on and Tabitha loved her new shawl.

"Milady, yours!"

"Thank you, Mrs West!" She had been spending her evenings embroidering handkerchiefs for presents. "They are lovely and so fine!" Milady gave her a kiss on the cheek

Ernest and Matilda gave Elizabeth a book, one she had been awaiting. "We know you like reading!"

Tabitha gave her a drawing of the house. "That's really good, you are talented!"

"Has anyone seen Dan this morning?"

"I heard him outside, he will be in for breakfast in a while."

"Well, when he does, he has presents here."

They all had a lovely day; food, games and laughter. Guests came and went, all keeping an eye on the snowy weather. And there were no tears from Amelia or Charles. "Come along now, you two, it is bed time!"

"Mama! Already?"

"It is later than usual, you two! We are visiting the cottages tomorrow, if the snow has not laid too thickly," said she, looking out at the continuous snow falling. We shall see, she mused.

The children were in bed, there were voices in the distance and laughter, "Another wedding in six days!" Loneliness crept in but she wouldn't let it stay. "They aren't leaving us, but if they wanted to… Well, we will cross that bridge, if we have to do so."

Next day was crisp and sunny. The snow lay and was quite deep in places.

"Are we going to see Matt?"

"What do you think Ernest?"

"If we keep to the path, it will be all right."

As they were getting coats and boots on, he whispered into Milady's ear, "Take your pistol with you!"

Something had to dampen the Christmas spirit. "Things have been quiet, too quiet, I am thinking," he added.

Lifting her bag up, as if he could see the little pistol sitting inside, she said, "I have the same feeling as you, but I've been trying not to think about it. It is Christmas!"

He looked at her, not saying what he was thinking. The children were paying attention to their conversation now.

Off they went in the carriage with the two horses. Ernest was on his horse, keeping a watchful eye; his demeanour was making her feel anxious. What did he know that he isn't telling? Pulling up at the cottages they saw the children old enough to stand were outside throwing snowballs.

"Can we play?"

"Yes you can but do not wander off!" Matt came out and gave Ernest a tankard of something. "Thank you, your good health!"

"Milady, Lottie's indoors with George." Tapping on the door, "Morning, Lottie," she called.

"Come in, Milady. Thank you for our presents, it's so kind of you!"

"Did you have a merry time?" said she, looking around the room and clearing a seat for herself.

"Would you like some mead, Milady?"

She did not really fancy mead but it would appear ungracious to refuse. "Yes please," she said. It was warm and surprisingly refreshing.

"Did Ernest tell ee, Milady, about strange lights around them there woods?"

"No, he hasn't," she replied, coming right back to reality. *So that's why he's been flustered,* she thought.

"Yes, the men have been taking turns on guard till he's been caught," said Lottie, getting up and checking on the children; the men were now playing a ball game with them.

Ernest came in. "It has started to snow again."

"Lottie, we had better go before it gets too thick," said Milady, finishing her drink. "We will see you all on New Year's Eve at church, then at my home for dinner."

The children were already in the carriage and tucked up. "Let's go home." She felt unnerved by the silence on the way; even the birds were quiet. Putting her hand in her bag she held her pistol for reassurance and swift action if required. The journey seemed long, she was seeing imaginary faces behind every bush, and arriving home she let out a sigh of relief.

"Ernest, I don't like this anxious feeling! I think we should hunt this person down, in the New Year, when the weather brightens up a bit, as he has the advantage at the moment he would see you and the men coming."

"Yes, we are making a plan to do the very same."

It was the day of the wedding. Ernest had stayed at Matt's cottage for the night so as not to see the bride before the wedding ceremony. All the household were attending the church, after the ceremony Mrs West would be rushing back to ensure all was ready. Her sister had engaged her friends to help in the kitchen while all else were at the church.

The little church was full; Ernest and Matilda were a popular couple. The music started and Matilda began walking up the aisle on the arm of her brother, her dress in cream which she had made herself went beautifully with her cream lacy hat and a bouquet of pink peonies. The couple placed their left hands on a little cushion the vicar was holding.

"Do you, Ernest William Wood, take Matilda Louise Tregathin to be your wife?

"Will you love her, comfort her, honour and protect her and forsaking all others be faithful to her as long as you both shall live?"

"I WILL."

Now looking at Matilda.

"Matilda Louise Tregathin, will you take Ernest William Wood to be your husband? Will you love him comfort him honour and protect him and forsaking all others be faithful to him as long as you both shall live?

"I WILL."

It was like seeing a brother getting married, Elizabeth reflected. The service was over and it was back to the house. Elizabeth had borrowed Mr Bennett's carriage for the occasion. Mr Bennett was there but not Sophia and Albert, who were still away somewhere in Europe. The little group crammed into the carriage, while Dan sat up front. Back at the house Ernest and Matilda were greeting everyone at the door with a glass of wine. Wine, mead and ale were flowing freely. Mrs West and her throng of helpers had done an amazing job.

The downstairs of the house was full, some people Milady knew, others were complete strangers. Once she began introducing herself as mistress of the happy couple, it turned out that they mostly were from nearby villages.

"Good day, I am Lady Tremaine." Hands were shaken. One man looked hesitant.

"This is my wife Ebrel and I am Credan; and this is our daughter Erwin."

Milady was smiling at them all. "Pray, how was your journey here?"

"The path was sludgy, making it slippery, but our old horse managed quite well. We'll be going soon, before it freezes. It is a lovely wedding, Milady!"

"Yes, and they are a lovely couple!" She was feeling tired; she was a hospitable host, but now she wished they would go, and as if they knew what she was thinking the crowds thinned out to a few stragglers.

Mr Bennett was on his way out. "Dear Elizabeth! A wonderful day, you did 'em proud!" he declared, kissing her hand. "Happy New Year, my dear!"

"And the same to you, Mr Bennett!" she called, as he stumbled out into the evening air which was biting at his extremities. He wrapped his scarf around his neck.

Back into the hallway and the house was theirs again. "My heartfelt congratulations again to you both! Here is the key to the little cottage at the back of the house." Ernest and Matilda looked surprised. "Yes, secretly and lovingly restored, it's your new home if you want it," said Milady, suddenly feeling silly, it never occurred to her they might have made their own plans!

They were looking at each other. "Thank you... Elizabeth!" exclaimed Ernest, enfolding her in his arms. Matilda hugged them both. "We didn't want to move away from here, with the new baby and all!"

The newlyweds were gone, even if only to the back of the house. The children were in bed and their mother had read to them. She herself was tired; she looked around, there were clothes everywhere. "It can wait till tomorrow," she murmured. Going downstairs a noise coming from the kitchen made the hairs on her arms stand up; she couldn't think who was in the house. She'd always had Ernest...now he would live in his own home. Hugo and Copper started to bark wildly. A door slammed downstairs. Looking over the banister she realised the candles were still lit, casting shadows. Seeing her bag on the table she ran down the last flight of stairs, got to it and thankfully her pistol was still there. Feeling braver now putting her bag across her body as a precaution.

A shot rang out.

The dogs were still barking, now growling and snarling. "Come here, Hugo!" speaking in a hoarse whisper. Hugo came first followed closely by Copper. Hugo had blood on his face. "Are you hurt?" she exclaimed, quickly examining him. "There are no cuts, so the intruder must be bleeding. Come on boys!"

Elizabeth made her way through the house, creeping along the corridors. The dogs barked and she jumped; a figure appeared in front of her and she pointed the pistol.

"Tt's me!" Ernest stood there.

"Dear Lord! I could have shot you!"

"We heard the dogs barking." Looking at Hugo, "What happened to him?" he exclaimed.

"I didn't shoot him! They were barking; a door slammed, and here we are!" said she, putting the pistol down.

"I will search the house. No windows are broken so they must have found a door open."

"Well, with the visitors here today, someone could have hidden until now and was missed."

"You wait here. Come on boys!" Hugo looked quite menacing with blood on his face. She could hear them walking around the house, finally in the kitchen

"All shut. I came though the scullery door; it was unlocked. There's blood over the handle. Look!"

"Well they have gone now. Thank you for investigating!" said she, as she wiped the blood off Hugo's snout. "You go now. Hugo won't rest tonight now they both have the run of the house. Is Dan in the grounds?"

"Yes, but a little worse for wear," said he, laughing.

"You go...we will be all right. I'll sleep with the children tonight." He was reluctant to go. "Ernest! Go to your wife! We will be safe." Whispering, she added, "And I have my pistol."

"I'll see you early in the morning!" He waved and was gone. She didn't doubt that, as they were both early risers, smiling to herself."

"Come on then, boys! Sleep...guard us well." Making a bed up on the chaise longue, Elizabeth fell asleep quickly.

The children woke early, bemused as to why their mama was sleeping in their room. Stretching, she said, "I was lonely, so I came in here with you!" Both hugged her. "Come along, then, let's have some breakfast." A smell drifted up the stairs. "Umm, bacon!"

"Mrs West, I didn't expect you here so early."

"Well, Milady; my little dears! I am used to getting up early, and thought I'd come along and make you all breakfast... What's all that blood by the door there?" she asked, nodding towards the doorway casually, as she turned the bacon over.

"Mama, where did that come from?" said Charles. The door handle turned, making Charles jump.

"Good morning Milady; 'morning all!" said Ernest, letting his new wife walk in first."

"Are you all right, Charles?"

"Have you seen that blood? I didn't realize there was so much." enquired Milady, pointing.

"Yes, I'll clean it up." Ernest disappeared then returned with a bucket, pouring hot water from the coal fire

"'Ere, don't use all the water!"

Ernest smiled. "I won't!" Later the children were in the conservatory with Tabitha, who said she had stayed with her family overnight. Milady had her doubts about that story, but who was she to question anyone?

"Well Ernest, who do you think the blood belongs to? The man in the woods and the highwayman could be one and the same. It has been over four months now."

"I'll ride over to the cottages later, Milady, and speak to Matt and whoever it was who fired the shot."

"When will you take your honeymoon?"

Matilda answered for them both. "'Tis not the weather for it, Milady, we'll wait till spring."

Ernest rode back with Matt. "No sign. He's a slippery one, that's for sure. Perhaps this time he is done for."

Milady was feeling worried. "Let's hope you are right and that's that!" All three of them looked at each other. "But let's be cautious."

An unsettling peace came over the area, as they all wanted to believe he was gone.

The weeks drifted into months; the season was changing; spring was around the corner and Sophia and Albert were back, but not for long. Albert was stationed in London so his dearest Sophia was to follow and fairly quickly, as they were going to be a threesome.

Mr Bennett couldn't be happier, but the day came for farewells. Milady's condition was obvious now, the true friends stood by her but the gossipmongers had a 'field day', especially over who the father might be. Ernest was top of the list. He was his usual self, "Ignore, and they will find someone else to slander." She was shunned in the street but she kept her head up, and felt nothing for them but pity for being so small-minded; she could do nothing else. She knew this would happen if she played with fire, she would not get burnt, just a little singed, perhaps.

"Elizabeth, I will be so sorry to leave you again! You will visit when your child is in this world?"

"Of course! I will bring all three up, we will need a little vacation, and to see you my dear friend!"

Sophia was gone and she felt lost again. Despite the menfolk finding no body after that awful night, she still went for her walks, usually taking Hugo with her. She wanted to be strong for the birth.

"Milady, should you be riding so late in your condition?"

"You mean I am too large?"

Ernest blushed. "No; well, I was thinking you might fall off."

"Ooh! Yes, you're right," said she, getting off the horse with as much decorum as she could manage.

She walked along the beach throwing sticks for Hugo, who jumped around like a pup. For a moment, she relaxed, then Hugo stopped, standing still he sensed something. "Hugo, what is it, boy?" Now feeling nervous she muttered, "Let's go home!" She did all but run, breathlessly getting to the house

"What is it?" asked Tabitha.

"Hugo's acting oddly so we came home! Check the doors, please," said she, looking at Matilda as she came into the kitchen to see what the noise was about. "Take Hugo with you." Locking the big oak door, she caught her breath. Someone tried the door, making her jump. "Who is it?"

"Ernest!"

She unlocked the door. "You have heard then?" said he.

"Heard what?"

"There's a stranger prowling again." Milady looked towards the door as though it was going to burst open. "He's not dead, is he? He wants revenge for me shooting him!"

"I don't know why, but he is still around, he's biding his time it seems for the opportune moment." So the peace was broken. "The militia are still nearby, but the military have gone to London."

"I wonder if that's why he is in the neighbourhood now?"

"I'll ride over to Mr Bennett's to inform him of the situation; as a magistrate he should know."

"Perhaps the military would come back."

"I don't think so, Milady, they were going to France."

"So we have to deal with this ourselves?"

"Yes, with the help of the militia, of course," said Ernest, thinking out loud.

"Lock up, Milady, I will not be long." And he was gone. She could hear the sound of a horse galloping off into the distance.

Time passed. All the adults felt uneasy. Matilda came into the study as Milady was at the window. "He's been gone a while, I hope he's all right!"

Not turning around, Milady murmured, "He did mention going to the cottages on the way back."

"It's raining again and getting dark." Now standing beside her at the window Milady put an arm around Matilda's shoulders. "He is a strong man and wily, like a fox."

"There! He's back!" Matilda pointed to a dark figure riding through the gate as though he had the wind up his tail.

Dismounting quickly and taking the horse to the stable he hurried to the front door, where both women were waiting. He rushed in, looking pale.

"Ernest, what's happened?"

Looking into the face of the woman he had protected all his adult life, he said, "There has been an attack at the cottages…"

She felt the bottom of her stomach fall out. "Who?"

He was fiddling with his hat and looking down. "Lottie's dead," he murmured. Milady felt suddenly faint; Ernest caught her and carrying her into the study laid her gently on the couch. Opening her eyes immediately her head touched the pillow, she whimpered, "Ooh, forgive me! I don't usually faint! George, is he," struggling for a word, "alright?"

Ernest interrupted her question. "No, he's fine. They think the man attacked her when she went outside around the cottage to get wood."

"Oh Lord, how is Matt?"

"He's out looking for blood, the rest have gone looking for him before he comes to harm, of course leaving some to guard the rest of the women and children."

Looking at her hands that were now cold, Milady quietly asked, "Do they know who it is?" She was looking up at Ernest and dreading the answer.

"The elusive prowler that's been lurking."

"We need to find him, don't we?"

"Yes we do, before he comes after you, Milady!"

"You think he will?"

"Yes. I am sure it's the highwayman you shot all those months ago. I think he made an attempt to get in, but Hugo got in the way." Hugo looked up when he heard his name and wagged his tail. "Good boy!" said Ernest, patting his head, "he has his scent now."

"Why Lottie?"

"I don't know. He was probably looking for someone to kill and she appeared."

Tears streamed down Milady's face. "Poor Lottie, and Matt, who has to live with this!"

Tabitha came in, putting a hand to her mouth as she heard the end of the conversation. "Oh no! Poor things!"

"I am all right now," said Milady, carefully sitting up and ignoring the sharp pain in her back. *Please, not now,* thinking to herself.

Ernest did not know what to say by way of comfort. "Come on, Hugo; Copper. I'll search before I go, stay indoors, Milady."

"It's all right, Ernest, we won't leave the house. It is checked and all is secure." Just as Ernest and Hugo were setting off he bent down to whisper to Milady, quietly when the other two were out of earshot, "Keep your pistol handy."

"As always!" Looking into his face and seeing emotion she hadn't perceived before, she was momentarily startled. "We will be fine, Ernest; go and catch this villain."

"I always do what I am asked, Milady," said he, and with a smile he was gone.

Her innards flipped. Was it the baby or her nerves? Copper, sensing the anxiety in the house, ran between the three women.

"I'll stay with the children upstairs and keep them occupied and safe."

"Thank you Matilda; we will keep watch down here. Where's Dan?"

"He went into the village for supplies; he should be back soon," said Tabitha as she peered out of the window. "'Tis shame Captain Edwards is away."

"Yes, we could do with him and his men right now."

The night drew in. The rain had stopped but a cold wind blew through the trees, making them look menacing, or was it their imagination? Tabitha was peering through the window. "What's that out there?"

"Merciful heavens, it's Dan! He's been injured! He was lying face down on the grass. I didn't see what happened," said Milady, peering through the window.

"It's a trap. You know what Ernest said, Milady, stay indoors!" said a frightened Tabitha, looking at Milady, afraid of what she would do.

"I know, but we can't leave Dan out there like that! There's been enough death today." An agonising few moments passed. "Tabitha, can you fire a pistol?"

"No Milady, but I can shoot a musket!" said she, looking pleased with herself.

"Right, this is what we'll do," said she, going into the kitchen to the place where the muskets were kept. Moments later Milady went out of the front door; it creaked as if it were warning her of her folly. She whispered loudly, "Dan, Dan!" No movement from Dan. *He's dead*, was her first thought. A wave of bravery went through her, resisting the urge to look around. "He's here, I can feel it."

"Ahh, there you are! I didn't think you'd let this young idiot die in the dirt!" The stranger appeared from the shadows.

Looking at his face, "So you are alive!" said she. He took a step towards her, limping.

"Yes missy, am alive, only just, nears lost my leg!" said he, holding the affected leg, "thanks to you," pulling a pistol out of a back pocket and waving it around. She hid hers in her dress pocket; she felt nervous and angry at the same time.

"Why did you kill that young woman?" He squinted, looking through pain-filled eyes.

"You hurt me, so I hurt you." She tasted nice, pretending to kiss the air; anyway, she saw me and got in the way. She had to die; enough of these pleasantries. Holding his gun with a slight tremor he pointed it, closing one eye as she took a deep breath. "I came to finish what I started," said he, continuing to point the gun.

"So then what? Are you leaving Cornwall?"

He pulled a knife from the other back pocket, lowering his gun arm.

"I know what you're doing, playing for time, missy! So who knocked you up?" He was using the gun to point. "The American? I presume he's long gone, dead is like."

An anger rose in her. *Keep calm, keep calm*, she said to herself. He lunged forward, catching her off guard, and lifted

117

his arm to fire, taking aim. Someone else nearby was taking aim. Her heart beating fast but her hands stayed firm. Milady found her voice. "Christmas day," a shot rang out as Milady threw herself onto the ground putting her hands over her head as protection.

Clutching his chest, he fell to the ground. Scrambling back onto her feet, Milady cautiously walked over to his apparently lifeless body.

He opened his eyes and coughed blood. "Well I be d–d," he muttered.

"Yes, you will be!" She took aim and shot him in the heart. He was dead for Lottie.

Tabitha appeared from her hiding spot around the side of the house and the women hugged each other. "Well done! You saved both our lives! Once he'd shot me, he would have probably come in the house to make his revenge complete!"

She bent down to a stunned Dan, who was rubbing his head.

"What happened?"

"Tabitha's a good shot, she saved us!" Copper came out barking and running around.

"Really! A girl! Should have let Copper out."

"No! Tabitha needed a clear shot, Copper would have made him move around!"

"Yes, Dan," said Milady, helping him up, then a wave of pain shot though her body. Clutching her abdomen, "It's too early!" she cried.

Matilda came out. "Tabitha, look after the little ones please, come on now Milady, it's your time; it's early but we can't stop nature." She put her arm around her shoulders.

Ernest came galloping in with a few riders behind him and they dismounted.

"All's well!" shouted Dan as he held his head.

"Where is everyone?" Looking down at the bloody body Matt got his gun out. Ernest placed a hand on his. "He's dead, friend; it's done."

A scream was heard, and all looked up at the first floor window. "I must see what's going on!" Ernest ran upstairs with a couple of men behind him to be met by Mrs West, hurrying as much as her frame would allow towards Milady's bedroom. She looked at the men, towels in her arms.

"It's the baby!"

"Can I do anything?"

"Fetch old Doc from the village." He was back down the stairs and as he reached the bottom stair the front door was open, the body still lying there for all to see. Matt was still standing over the body.

"Come on now, Matt, I have to go to get the doc."

Matt looked into Ernest's face. "What will I do now, Ernest?" he murmured.

"You'll bring up that little boy!" said Ernest, patting his back.

A light suddenly shone in his face. "Go! You must go, I have to see my son!" Ernest galloped out of the courtyard. Dan was up and about, still rubbing his head and feeling embarrassed at being caught off guard.

The labour was long, two days of walking around at all hours, with both dogs walking after her, not knowing why their mistress would suddenly stop and clutch her bulging stomach, and cling onto something for support while trying not to cry. Amelia and Charles thought Mama was acting strange. As Matilda explained, "The baby's coming!" a worried little girl looked up.

"I am never having a baby if it makes you walk around like this!" Matilda was trying not to smile, but feeling very much the same way.

"It's worth it in the end, your mama had the both of you."

Finally the last stage came, Milady staggered into her bedroom looking like a women possessed. "Tabitha, it's time!" she gasped between spasms of pain. Isabelle Marie was born, small, but with a good pair of lungs. There was a knock at the door.

"Come in!"

"I heard a baby was born!" exclaimed Ernest.

Looking down into the little screwed-up face, "Yes, she made her entry into the world known!" said Milady, laughing.

"Are you all right?"

In a tired voice, "Yes, thank you Ernest," she murmured.

"Some flowers from Matt," said he, holding them out.

Tabitha took them. "I'll put them in water."

Wiping a tear from her face, "How is he?" she asked.

"Better now that fiend is dead. Mr Bennet sends his regards, with flowers and much else downstairs."

"Thank you Ernest, let's hope now we can start to live without looking over one shoulder, and you two can have that honeymoon of yours!"

"We couldn't leave till everything was resolved."

"Well, all is resolved now, and who'd have thought Tabitha was such a good shot? I don't know quite what would have happened!"

"You should have all stayed indoors and shot from a window," said a frustrated Ernest, "or let Copper out to distract him!"

"The silly dog would have been hurt," she retorted, hugging her baby girl close, Isabelle's finger wrapped around hers. Now she looked up into Ernest's face.

"Dear friend! It's done now."

Relaxing, "Yes I suppose it is," said he, and now smiling, "any names yet, Milady?"

"Say hallo to Isabelle Marie Tremaine."

"I gather after her grandmother?"

"Yes, and Isabelle after the woman who brought me up as her own; my life could have been so very different."

It took a few weeks of cosseting by the women in the household for Milady to be back on her feet and feeling her old self, but she felt something was missing. She had a good life with three beautiful healthy children. Spring was in the air, babies were being born to all mammals, trees had come back to life with birds weaving in and out of the branches, chirping away as they went. Even the peacocks sounded happy to be out and about in the warmer air.

"I am going to the beach, Matilda."

"Are you sure you're well enough, Milady?"

"Yes, I'll take Hugo and Copper with me. I need fresh air, I won't be long!" Freedom without the restrictions that winter brought, thinking to herself.

Wrapping her woollen shawl around her shoulders, her hair loose, she walked along the beach path, feeling relaxed but still resisting the temptation to look over her shoulder. There was a sudden noise in the sky; the birds were squabbling. Smiling, she said aloud, "Elizabeth, stop it!" then looked around to see if anyone was there. "With me talking to myself they'll cart me off to Bodmin asylum!"

The dogs both went for a swim, making her laugh. Copper had grown so much he was taller than his mentor now, and was still growing. Both dogs ran ahead, and she hastened to catch up. Then they started barking and her senses quickened. A short rang out, she turned around, in time to see a man fall, still holding a very large knife! She clutched her chest, frozen on the spot. There was a rustle in the bushes; a man jumped out.

"You all right, Milady?" Astonished, she was now looking into the eyes of Matt!

"Yes, yes! I think I am thanking you for my life!" Elizabeth threw herself into his arms; he didn't know quite how to respond and she stepped back. "It's so lucky you were here!"

"Well, not so; Ernest told us to follow you on your walks, Milady. He was afraid there was a second man, and that the highwayman must have had a partner to look after him all those months. And he was right, we think you can relax now!"

"I hope so," said she smiling, and she set off with a quickened step, looking around as she went. The dogs were running between Matt and the body and her. In the courtyard, she spoke to Ernest. "Matt will need your help, we have another dead body."

Looking sheepish, "I didn't tell you, I thought it would make you nervous," he said, "but we didn't leave you unprotected."

"Thank you, Ernest, your plan has succeeded! Is there anything else I should know now?"

"No, none of which I am aware!" He pulled his cap on securely and got on the cart. Waving, he called, "I'll go to help Matt," and through the gates he was gone.

Matilda met her at the door. "Are you all right, Milady?"

"Yes, the second man has been killed... You don't looked surprised!"

"Well, Ernest warned me to be vigilant."

"Matt shot him as he was going to stab me!"

"We thought it would be too much for you to deal with after the birth of little Isabelle."

"Yes I have been relaxed," said she, not wanting to speak of missing Charles.

"I expect Mr Charles will soon be back safe and sound." Milady looked astonished. "Is there anything you don't know?"

Matilda was blushing and smiling. "Well, Milady, you've had his child, you must have loved him to make her, so I was thinking you miss him."

"Yes, you're right... I do miss him," she murmured, touching Matilda's clutched hands. Walking into the conservatory she was greeted by her two eldest children.

"Mama!"

She wrapped her arms around them. "Have I ever told you how much I love you both?"

Now they were giggling. "Mama, you are tickling!"

"Matilda is back, time for lessons. I will see you at tea time."

Lottie's funeral was as expected a solemn affair. Women were trying to sob quietly, the older woman holding George was wiping her eyes. George looked and started crying too, his little world was upside down and he didn't understand why. Matt gave the eulogy, having to stop halfway to compose himself. Lottie was buried in the little church graveyard, her grave facing the rising sun. "She loved the sun!" he explained, looking away, wiping the tears from his face.

The following weeks went quickly and quietly. The children were allowed outside on the lawn, playing some game with the dogs. There was laughter and barking, and Isabelle chuckling when anyone paid her any attention. One day a horse and carriage pulled into the driveway. Milady got up from her comfortable sitting position to greet the visitor.

"Mr Bennett, how pleasant to see you!"

"My dear, and you looking so well, after all the unwelcome excitement."

"Yes, it has been a tiring time! Any news from Sophia and Albert?"

"Yes, only what I do expect. You know all is well. Sophia is doing well, the baby is due in three months' time."

"The time will fly by."

"I have news from a certain Mr Charles..." feeling herself blush.

"Is he well? When is he coming back?"

"Now now, my girl! He is safe and will be back soon. He has some business to clear up first."

Looking into his face she knew he knew more, but wouldn't or couldn't say.

"I will just have to be patient, although it will be hard as it is not in my nature!" said she laughing, and putting her arm into his. "Now sir, would you like a drink?"

"Don't mind if I do!" he chortled. All manner of topics were discussed. Ernest joined them and Elizabeth poured him a drink.

"Is Albert back from France yet?"

"Yes, but not for long. There is trouble there and it is going to affect us. There is an agitator who is rallying those poor starving people to rebel. I don't know the full details so I cannot comment further... Anyway, my dear, delightful to see you looking so well. I must be off," said he, groaning as he got up, "these legs have seen better days." Leaning heavily on his stick he hobbled out into the sunshine. The children were being ushered indoors.

"Mrs West has cooked us a delicious tea!" As if on cue the smell caressed their nostrils. "Well, Ernest, it looks like some sort of war, another civil war, the saddest kind."

He looked deep in thought but said nothing. Tea finished, it was time to read to the children. "What book would you like?" asked their mama, hoping it was not 'Goody Two-Shoes' again.

"The 'Little Jack' book, Mama, please."

"A different one, a pleasure," she murmured. As usual they fell asleep just into the first few pages.

Looking out of her bedroom window the peacocks were strutting around, the moon was bright and the air was warm. A slight breeze made her shudder. Feeling suddenly tired, she got into her fresh sheets, stretching out and within minutes she too, was fast asleep. Isabelle was asleep in her crib next to her mother's bed.

A figure lurked in the shadows. "Tomorrow, Milady!"

Chapter Nine

Elizabeth stretched her arms over her head as she climbed out of bed. "Hush, Isabelle!" said she, picking the screaming baby up and putting her to her breast, with an immediate reaction of silence. Nice smells wafted up the stairs making her stomach rumble. "It seems I am hungry, too!" The baby was fed and changed.

"Good morning, everyone!" Tabitha took Isabelle from Milady and placed her in her crib. "Is anything planned for today?"

Ernest looked up. "I am in the fields with Matt, making hay while the sun shines," said he, smiling. "And you, Milady?"

"I think I will take a walk along the beach." She was waiting for a reaction.

Matilda looked up. "Will you be taking the children, Milady?"

"Yes. Fresh air will do them good."

"I will come too, begging your pardon, Milady, I need fresh air." She smiled at Matilda. And my pistol will be a safeguard, she reflected. After breakfast Charles's shirt was changed as most of his food was down his front.

No coats were needed, just hats. Isabelle was wrapped up and with a shawl secured to Milady's chest. *While she is so small, I can do this,* Milady thought to herself. I saw pictures in my books and those women were working like this, so I am sure I can walk along the beach.

It was dry and the sun was behind the clouds. The two children ran freely, stopping every so often to gaze at the treasure the sea had washed in. Admiring pieces of smooth green glass, they were looking up into the sky through the glass. "Mama, look! Green sky!"

Taking the glass from his little hands she looked up at the sky. "You're right, Charles!" scrutinising the area though the green haze. A figure on a horse cantered towards them. A sudden panic caught in her throat. "Matilda, Matilda!" she shouted, moving towards her and looking around frantically to ascertain the children's whereabouts. "I don't recognise the rider." It was a tall figure, his coat blowing out behind him. "Is it Charles?"

Matilda was squinting and holding a hand over her eyes. "You're right, Milady, 'tis Mr Charles." Milady, hardly able to contain herself, now felt nervous. Isabelle stirred. "It's your papa!" she whispered.

The horse slowed as it approached the ladies. He jumped down and walked towards Milady leading the horse behind him.

"Elizabeth!" he murmured, touching her face and pushing her hair back, not noticing the little bundle attached to her chest. Taking her in his arms and kissing her mouth, he was all too aware the children were there. Elizabeth whispered into her mouth, "Hello..." her insides stirred like butterflies fluttering just as Isabelle decided to stretch. "Good God! Hello, little one," touching her hair. Realisation dawned on him; he was looking shocked.

"Meet Isabelle, your daughter."

Touching her silky brown hair, "Oh, my darling!" he cried, then kissing the baby's head, "I am sorry I left when I did!" now hugging them both gently.

"Can we hug too?" Amelia and Charles joined in hugging the adults' legs, while Matilda was content to stroke the horse, smiling. *At last!* she thought to herself.

They were walking and talking all at once, the children excited, running ahead with Matilda. Hugo saw them coming towards the gate and ran to meet them, his floppy ears covering his eyes, his tongue hanging out; Copper followed in hot pursuit.

"Hello boys!" said Charles, stroking their heads.

"Hugo still knows you!" Elizabeth laughed as both dogs ran around excitable and sniffing Charles' legs and coat.

"Steady on boys!" he commanded, then they wagged their tails.

"Mr Bennett tells me there has been upheaval while I have been away."

"When did you see him?"

"Late last night. I rode past your house but it was late and I wanted our first meeting to be at the right time."

Looking from his face to the green grass Elizabeth said, "Yes, there has been death and murder... Oh, I nearly shot your messenger, and the snow! Let's not forget how cold it has been. Was there snow where you were?"

"Yes, he told me," said he smiling, "I know what you want to know. We'll talk later in private," he added, kissing her mouth.

Isabelle opened her eyes, yawned and went back to sleep. Indoors, luncheon was eaten, while Ernest and Charles talked about farming, and he looked mesmerised at the little face on his lap. Ernest continued, "Yes we have planted; in fact we have taken advantage of the weather."

"I must liaise with my steward, and of course Mr Bennett; he has been kind enough to oversee while I have been away."

The children were with Matilda in the conservatory, while Charles and Elizabeth were now in the study with a glass of wine.

"I have a letter from the woman who gave birth to you," said he, handing her a heavy embossed envelope with a seal. She stared at the seal as though she was afraid of the contents, "I will leave you to read it." He put his glass down and walked out of the French windows into the now glorious sunshine. Opening the letter gingerly, a ring fell out, a rose-cut diamond cluster ring. Holding it in her palm, and mesmerised by the writing she began to read.

"My darling Elizabeth I have trusted your friend Mr Charles Long with this letter as secrecy is of the paramount.

I am sorry we never grew to know one another, and now we never will. My country is in turmoil and I do not think it is safe to travel, me to you or you to visit me, for shortly I will have to leave my beloved country, never to return.

I have enclosed a little token of my love for you. I only held you in my arms for a short while but you are in my heart forever. For both our safeties, your father took you home to Cornwall where dear Isabelle brought you up as her own.

Do not think ill of your father and me for keeping such a secret, we thought it best at the time, and from what I hear from my friends overlooking you all your life we acted for the best.

Live long and happy, my child!

With all my love and affection,

Your mother

Marie Adelaide, of the House of Bourbon."

There was a fleur-de-lis embossed motif at the end of the page. She read the letter again and put the ring on, which fitted perfectly. Charles came back in; wiping a tear away she looked up at him. "What is she like?"

"You are very much like her in looks and temperament. Dark hair and likes riding, I am sure in her younger days she was climbing trees!" They both laughed.

"I found a picture of her in a book; is she in such peril?"

"She is safe at present, but she made an enemy of her nephew's wife, and there is a rumour of an uprising by the people against the royal family," seeing her face, "but she is safe," seeing the look on her face and changing the subject, "and the highwayman was killed."

"Yes, by Tabitha, well... And me," said she, looking down and feeling embarrassed as she'd shot his cousin.

"And his accomplice!" Peace at last. She could barely believe it, and was almost afraid to say it.

"No one left to shoot!" said she laughing, "And I like it that way!"

Suddenly he was in front of her, kissing her passionately; catching his breath he proposed, "I love you! Will you be my wife?"

"Yes, yes!" cried she, flinging her arms around his neck. He picked her up and whirled her around till they were both dizzy.

"Are you going away again?"

"No, my business in France was to secure your mother."

"But how did you know her?" she asked, thinking of his next words carefully.

"It was Mr Bennett's business and he asked me to protect her and move her to a safer location. They had kept in contact since your father died. He took over your father's task as your protector, as your father wished."

"All this was going on behind my back!"

"Are you annoyed?"

"No and yes! If I had known of her existence, I would have probably done something dangerous to us both."

"Well, when are you making an honest woman of me?"

"As soon as possible! Will that stop us going upstairs?" said he, raising his eyebrows.

Laughing and falling into his arms, "No, it won't, but the children will!" she declared.

When the house was quiet the three of them were in the study, drinking a toast to everything that came to mind.

"Well, goodnight Milady, Charles; I have a long day tomorrow."

"Goodnight Ernest," they both echoed.

"You don't treat him like a servant."

"He isn't! He's my best friend and like a brother; I couldn't imagine a life without him in it."

Ernest, just the other side of the door, smiled.

It was the day of the wedding. Sophia, now great with child, made it home but Albert was off on some mission in France.

Arm in arm they walked up the aisle, Ernest gave Milady's hand to Charles.

"Look after her."

"I will."

The service went without a hitch and even the children stayed quiet.

"I pronounce you man and wife." Then came the kiss and the congregation clapped in delight. "Congratulations to you both!"

Only a few people had been invited to the church; after immediate family, friends and the cottage folk, there was a handful from the village. Milady felt shame due to Isabelle's birth and people snubbing her, but the church doors opened to a large gathering of people who had seemingly forgotten their prejudices as they threw rice and wished the couple well, with everyone else making Milady smile.

People can be so gloriously unpredictable, she thought to herself, but she didn't care; that day she was really happy. The summer was hot, the land was fertile and it wasn't long before Milady was expecting again and Matilda announced that she, too, was carrying a child.

"Oh, Sophia! How are you?" Her friend was holding a little bundle, tired but happy.

"Albert comes home soon."

"How are you feeling?" asked Sophia, both looking down at a growing bulge. Elizabeth put a protective hand on her unborn child.

"It is different this time, I don't have to hide my condition."

"And how's Matilda keeping?"

"We have cut down her time with the children, so she can rest."

"Will you be hiring someone else?"

"In the short time while she's recovering." Albert came back safe with news of France. It seemed he was wrong; it hadn't quietened down as he thought. *Yes, I know,* thought Milady, but it was her secret and she couldn't tell her friend.

Two men were standing in the study looking out onto the garden, watching a family scene; there was Milady, Charles, Amelia and Master Charles, and of course Isabelle in her perambulator. Ernest felt melancholy, especially when the two eldest played pirates, chasing each other around the same tree their mother did with him, all those years ago.

"So it's done, she is safe for the immediate future." Both were taking sips from their brandy glasses.

"Does she know?"

"It would serve no purpose," said Ernest, taking a large gulp and pouring another glass. "And you?" he added, holding the decanter up to Mr Bennett.

"I don't mind if I do."

"This could all have been yours," said he, looking at Mr Bennett squarely in the face. "I am the Tremaine bastard, and anyway I like my life the way it is; I have family and a woman to love, and a roof over my head."

"Elizabeth has always thought of me like a brother, and I like that feeling."

Mr Bennett was looking at Ernest's profile. "So was it you who, um, brought into line the wayward husband?" looking into an expressionless face, "He had an accident, if he would get blind drunk after a night with his mistress." Face lightens, "His carelessness was about to lose them their home," looking at Mr Bennett, "and I could not allow that."

"So if Mr Long crosses the line?"

"Let's hope he doesn't. I think she would shoot him, anyway."

"Sir, you are a gentleman!" Ernest smiled. Mr Bennett held up his glass.

"Milord!"

CPSIA information can be obtained
at www.ICGtesting.com
Printed in the USA
BVHW042312021218
534619BV00010B/50/P

9 781787 102347